Ouachita River Valley
Courtesy of: USGS

Cedar Glades Express

By
Janis Kent Percefull
Arkansas Historian

Author of

Non-Fiction
Ouachita Springs Region: A Curiosity of Nature

Fiction
Three Strangers Come To Call

With Illustrations by
Erin E. Holliday

Published by
Muscadine Press LLC
Benton, Arkansas 72018

Copyright © 2010 by Janis Kent Percefull
Illustrations by Erin Holliday

All rights reserved. No part of this book may be reproduced in whole or in part without written permission from the publisher, except by reviewers who may quote brief excerpts in connection with a review in a newspaper, magazine, or electronic publication; nor may any part of this book be reproduced, stored in a retrieval system, or transmitted in any form or by any means electronic, mechanical, photocopying, recording, or other, without written permission from the publisher.

Library of Congress Control Number: 2010936726

Percefull, Janis Kent
Cedar Glades Express/ by Janis Kent Percefull:
Illustrated by Erin E. Holliday

Summary: The renowned health resort and spa of Hot Springs, Arkansas endured a harsh winter, followed by numerous fires, and a major smallpox epidemic in the early weeks of 1895- decimating the local economy. In a plan to help their family, the MacNeil cousins Rachel Lee and Henrietta along with their friends Jake, Henry, and Max travel to the nearby village of Cedar Glades.

ISBN- 978-0-9830006-0-0

1.Historical fiction-adventure. 2.Hot Springs, Arkansas-1895. 3.Water Cure 4.Smallpox. 5.Civil War. 6.Strap Line Railroads. 7.Ouachita River Valley. 8.Cedar Glades, Arkansas.

Printed in the United States of America

With love
to

Aiden, Christopher, Columbia, Nova Lee, Patrick,
and Skyler

The Future

Acknowledgments

With considerable gratitude for their copious help in researching the 1895 smallpox epidemic in Hot Springs, Arkansas I acknowledge my indebtedness to Liz Robbins, Gail Ashbrook and the rest of the wonderful volunteers of the Garland County Historical Society.

In addition the Ellsworth papers from the University of Arkansas archives and the local history archives of the Garland County Library were especially valuable in reconstructing the smallpox epidemic.

Also, the archives of the National Weather, Forestry and Park Services, along with the USGS have been most helpful in recreating the physical environment of 1895 Hot Springs, Arkansas and the larger Ouachita springs region.

As ever, a special recognition of my Aunt Claire Lee Sims, whose keen insights, knowledge of Hot Springs history and skills as a copy editor has been indispensible.

And, I am deeply grateful to my publisher, John Archibald, for his tireless efforts to support my work with wonderful constructive edits, indispensible suggestions, and constant encouragement.

Contents

Time Line	vii, ix
Introduction	x

Chapter
1 Pandemonium	11
2 Cleaning	30
3 Woodbine Street	38
4 The Laundry	45
5 Soap Art	54
6 The Inoculation	60
7 The End of Quarantine	69
8 Reservation Piglet	76
9 Cedar Glades Association	87
10 On The Road to Cedar Glades	95
11 First Night in Camp	109
12 Clearing the Tracks	123
13 Home to the Farm	130
Glossary of Terms	136
National Historic People and Places	139
1890's Hot Springs, AR. City Directory	142
Advertisements	144
Meteorological Register	145
Hot Springs City Council Meeting	146
Newspaper Article	147

General Time Line

April 20, 1832
—Hot Springs Reservation established.

October 16, 1859
—John Brown seized the federal armory at Harpers Ferry in Virginia.

1862
—Union forces took possession of the Winchester and Potomac Railroad.

1876
—Supreme Court affirms federal government's claim to Ouachita thermal springs and surrounding area.

March 3, 1877
—Congress authorizes Hot Springs, Arkansas Reservation.

1890's
—Sanitation and personal hygiene era.

—Procter and Gamble Company starts a new advertising campaign for Ivory Soap that emphasizes, "It Floats."

Mid-1890s
—Women's editions of daily newspapers during this period involved a periodic, one day takeover, by women, of an entire newspaper. Besides news and editorials there were lavish illustrations and numerous advertisements.

February 5-7, 1895
—Winter blizzard blankets U.S. from Maine to Texas and from Wyoming to Washington D. C.

1893- 1897
—United States Depression

1895 Hot Springs Smallpox Time Line

February 10, Secret experiments to manufacture an effective smallpox serum in St. Louis become public.

February 22, Fire destroys a large residential and business portion of the town.

February 24, Malvern, Arkansas quarantines trains from Hot Springs.

February 26, Hundreds of visitors dashed to the "through" train to St. Louis. It was the only train allowed to breach the Malvern quarantine.

March 1, Hot Springs City Council addresses problems related to "recent large fire."

—Mrs. Fitzsimmons request payment from City Council for destruction of bedding due to smallpox.

March 7, Hot Springs City Council passes ordinance to regulate movement of persons from infected places and appropriating money for the suppression of smallpox.

March 31, Twenty-seven dead and 118 active cases of smallpox.

April 5, Office of City Physician created.

April 16, Mrs. Sarah Ellsworth writes her son Frank in Chicago that citizens of Hot Springs were scratching around for money to live on until the following spring.

May 1, City Council calls for purchase of land to be used as a pauper graveyard and for a contagious disease hospital.

May 12, Mrs. Sarah Ellsworth writes to her son Frank in Chicago that she only has "a suggestion of a garden left."

May 27, Hot Springs schools close for the summer.

Introduction

In the United States the 1890s was a time of great wealth and great poverty. Moreover, those who were affluent were not afraid to flaunt their wealth. For this reason Mark Twain dubbed it the Gilded Age. This term was a reference to covering a lily with gold, considered an ostentatious display of wealth.

Many Americans in this era viewed Hot Springs, Arkansas, as the nation's health resort as well as a fashionable spa. For these reasons both the wealthiest and the poorest citizens of the country came to Hot Springs. Thus, the economic life blood of the town relied on the constant arrival of visitors, especially during the cooler months from January through June. But a protracted national depression, a harsh winter, and numerous local fires followed by a major smallpox epidemic in the early weeks of 1895, decimated the local economy as visitors stayed away.

It is also likely that the larger Ouachita Springs Region was also impacted by these events. This larger community included several cold water resorts and numerous farming communities that relied on the Hot Springs and cold water resort markets for their products.

One of these outlying communities was the village of Cedar Glades, a few miles west of Hot Springs and a mile north of the Ouachita River.

Chapter 1

Pandemonium

The muffled knocking of hot steam on the cold radiator awakened Rachel Lee into consciousness. Uncle Samuel must have filled the boiler—and some time ago—since the coal was burning fiercely enough for the water to produce steam. Her uncle, Samuel MacNeil, had charge of tending to the boiler at the family boarding house on Market Street and Prospect Avenue. But she couldn't figure out why he fired up the boiler in the middle of the night?

Usually, he did that only in the dead of winter, if there were real cold weather. On those nights, she and her cousin, Henrietta, cracked open a window, as their bedroom on the third floor received more than its share of the steam-generated heat. This time of year, however, Uncle Samuel would fire the boiler early in the morning, then return to bed. By the time he and the rest of the household got up, the chill would be off the house.

Rachel Lee's morning duty was to fire up the kitchen stove. As such, she was always aware of the morning temperature. Or any unusual occurrences in the boarding house early in the morning. She began to drift asleep again as she recalled this past winter. Uncle Samuel attended to the boiler in the middle of the night for most of December, all of January, and half of February. Even the old-timers said that they had never known such a bitterly cold winter. Later, it would be known as the "Great Blizzard of 1894-1895" that hit much of the country including Arkansas. Rumor had it that the official thermometer up at the Army and Navy Hospital broke last month when the temperature fell below zero.

Again, the radiator clanged to life, louder and angrier than before. Rachel Lee was alerted back to the present. Something unusual was happening. It didn't feel like she had been in bed long enough for it to be morning. It was the middle of the night on March 4, and she was sure the bitter cold weather had broken over two weeks ago. Fully awakened now, Rachel Lee heard the frantic rattle of carriages and the fast paced clip-clop, clip-clop of horse hooves in the street. The usual pre-dawn chirps and twitter were absent. In their stead were deep pitched commands from driver to horse, and even higher pitched shrieks and cries. This clanging racket from outside mingled with the faint sound of voices rising from downstairs rooms of the boarders.

"Is it time to get up?" Henrietta croaked from her bed across the room, still half asleep.

"I don't think so," Rachel Lee replied.

"I wonder what's happening?" asked Henrietta. Her bed stood on the side of the room closest to West Mountain and Prospect Avenue, closer to the door and radiator. She got hot first when all the boarding house radiators warmed. The family called Henrietta and Rachel Lee's bedroom the Tower Room because the belfry of the house was above their bedroom. In fact, a little door in the ceiling of the bedroom led to the belfry. The family rang the bell once a year, on Independence Day.

"Did you hear that?" Henrietta said.

"Sure did," Rachel Lee replied, as she jumped out of bed and raced toward Henrietta's side of the room. Together, they opened the window, placed their bare hands on the sill and leaned out the window. Beneath them, five carriages raced past and headed toward Central Avenue. A light frost covered the treetops, but the girls didn't notice.

"They're not supposed to do that," Henrietta declared. "Racing in town is against the law." She was wide awake now. Usually it took Henrietta a good long time to shake off the strong arms of slumber. But nothing at the moment seemed usual. In fact, nothing in the past two weeks had been normal.

Before the carriages rolled out of sight, both girls heard more sounds on the east side of the house, facing Market Street plaza. They raced across to Rachel Lee's side of the room, flung the window open and looked with wide-eyed excitement at the sight below. From their vantage point on the third floor of the family's boarding house, they had a bird's-eye view of the scene below.

"What in the world ..." Rachel Lee said, as her jaw dropped.

"Holy cow!" Henrietta exclaimed.

The whole town had come alive. A sense of urgency filled the cold night air. The clatter of wagons and carriages of every type could be heard racing up, down and across every street and avenue for blocks around.

The early spring blizzard had delayed the busy season, but now the town overflowed with visitors. Health-seekers arrived all year long to take the water-cure in the famous Ouachita thermal springs. Spring ranked as the town's busiest time because health-seekers and pleasure-seekers poured into the Spa City.

Everyone in town depended financially on the spring season to see them through the rest of the year. In some way or another, every business had a connection to the bathing industry.

Rachel Lee looked out her bedroom window every day, except when the family visited their cottage near the village of Cedar Glades west of Hot Springs. She had never seen such a sight like the one unfolding before her.

From their window perch, the girls saw straight down to the circular-watering trough in the middle of Market Street plaza and many of the storefronts surrounding the square. Beyond the square to their left, a good slice of the city lay before them, especially the town's main district and the Federal Reservation. On the right, to the south, was their part of town, the Market Street plaza neighborhood.

Rachel Lee looked at her neighborhood, saddened by what she saw and remembered. Two weeks ago, a big fire destroyed four-and-a-half blocks along Ouachita Avenue toward Olive Street. Some people believed the fire started at Mr. Ledgerwood's Bakery, on account of the oven being too hot. Rachel Lee remained unconvinced. She thought like many of the people in the neighborhood that someone started it on purpose like the other fires a few days earlier. The wind blew strong that night and right up toward Market Street and Prospect Avenue. She and Henrietta, along with their grandmother and a permanent boarder, Miss Hurley, watched in horror as dozens of buildings burned up in gigantic yellow and orange flames within minutes. Their grandfather and Uncle Samuel had tried to help, but even the firemen had to run for their lives and lost their hoses to the fire.

"This is really strange," Rachel Lee stated out loud in a matter-of-fact way. She then grabbed the extra quilt that lay on one end of the window seat and covered herself and her cousin.

"There isn't this much excitement in the air on Saturday morning market day with all the farmers and their wagons and teams filling up the square."

Henrietta nodded in agreement and pulled the quilt closer around her shoulders.

In the pre-dawn darkness, the two 11-year-old cousins looked like two peas in a pod. But daylight would reveal that Henrietta was much smaller, lighter complexioned and had very unmanageable curly strawberry blond hair with eyes the color of pewter. Rachel Lee, on the other hand, stood tall for her age. She had eyes the color of coal and a much darker complexion. Even though her hair also had curls, it was much more manageable.

"Look at all the lights!" Rachel Lee exclaimed in wonder. Except for the buildings along Ouachita Avenue where the fire had traveled, every light in the boarding houses, cottages and hotels burned brightly. The buildings with electric lights were the brightest. However, many of the establishments in the famous spa of Hot Springs, Arkansas, of 1895 still used gas lighting. The town looked lit up like a New Years' Eve bonfire to them.

"After the last two weeks," Henrietta stated, "I didn't think we would have any more excitement till after school lets out for summer."

"Me, too," Rachel Lee nodded. "And I won't ever forget those three strangers who came to see Grandfather."

"Me, neither."

The girls settled comfortably on the window seat and pulled their quilt tighter to block out the cold March wind.

"First there was that newspaperman from New York," Henrietta recounted. "What was his name?"

"Mr. Crane. Stephen Crane," Rachel Lee sighed in admiration. "Then Mr. Sawyer, the wheelchair man Grandfather knew from the war."

"Don't forget Mr. Bruce McPherson …"

"… from Ed-in-bur-rah, Scot-land," Rachel Lee said. The girls mimicked the high-tone visitor who had offered their grandfather, Dr. Robert MacNeil, a title and castle in Scotland.

Each of the visitors brought some excitement into the family's' life, but Rachel Lee had been the most thrilled with Mr. Crane.

For a moment, the girls watched in silence from their front row seat on the third floor, and then Rachel Lee spoke.

"I can't believe everybody has their lights on in the middle of the night."

"Everybody, but poor Mrs. Fitzsimmons."

"Yeah," Rachel Lee responded, and then pondered their neighbor's misfortune. Mrs. Fitzsimmons ran the Alhambra Hotel across Ouachita Avenue from the Alhambra Bath House. Her hotel stood two blocks down the hill so they easily saw whether her lights were on or off.

About a week ago, at bedtime, Rachel Lee noticed all the lights were off at the Alhambra Hotel. Her hotel catered to businessmen, so the Alhambra Hotel always shone lights when the girls went to bed. But for a week now the hotel lacked lights. They tried to find out what happened. Nobody would say. They had been given strict instructions to avoid the Alhambra Hotel.

"Listen to that. Everyone sounds so frantic," Rachel Lee spoke with concern.

"Let's go see if Papa is up," Henrietta suggested, with a little tremor in her voice.

"Good idea."

Normally, they sought out their grandparents' room at such a time as this, but with the steam heat going full blast they figured Samuel would be the member of the family most likely to be awake and know what was going on.

After closing the windows, each girl wrapped herself in a dark grayish-blue heavy wool robe, identical except in size. They hurried down the special stairway from their bedroom to the second floor where the boarders stayed. Light showed through the glass transoms above the doors of the boarder's rooms on both sides of the hallway, except for Miss Amber Hurley. Miss Hurley's room was next to the stairway that led up to Rachel Lee and Henrietta's bedroom.

Mr. Salmon, the dry goods salesman from Memphis, and Mr. Bartholomew, the French cotton merchant from New Orleans, had their room lights on but the girls couldn't hear anything. Down the hall a ways, they stopped in front of the Graves' door. The Graves came from Missouri. Mr. Graves needed the Hot Springs baths for his rheumatism.

The girls heard the couple talking but couldn't understand them. Mrs. Graves sounded awfully frightened. This made the girls even more nervous and spurred them to run down the stairs, whiz through the dining room and burst into the kitchen, causing Samuel to spill coffee down his front.

"Have mercy you two!" Samuel sputtered, frantically grabbing a napkin to dab himself.

The girls were too frightened to consider they had just scared an adult into pouring coffee on himself, and drew closer to the man they viewed as an island of safety.

"What's going on Papa? Everyone's lights are on," Henrietta questioned.

"And it's the middle of the night," Rachel Lee added as she looked up at the big Regulator clock over the kitchen door that read 3:18 a.m.

Samuel took a deep breath. "Calm down, there's enough panic going on all around without us losing our heads. Sweet Pea," he calmly instructed his daughter, Henrietta, "get some cups. Honey," he nodded to Rachel Lee, "you get the cocoa powder and sugar. There's hot milk on the stove, fix yourself a cup and come sit down. I have a lot to tell you."

"Hot chocolate in the middle of the night, before school on Monday ... something is really wrong!" Rachel Lee spoke in a loud whisper to Henrietta as they scurried past the stove and entered the pantry. The cousins helped themselves to the cocoa powder and sugar, and then poured the hot milk into the mixture.

Carefully stirring their hot chocolate, they moved toward the kitchen table on the other side of the room between the kitchen sink and the back door that led to the screened-in back porch. Rachel Lee slid across the built-in bench opposite Uncle Samuel, with the windows at her back. Henrietta sat in a chair on her father's side and scooted as close to him as possible.

"I figured you girls would be up as soon as you heard all the commotion," Uncle Samuel began. "Now here's the situation ..."

Uncle Samuel, like their grandparents, was by nature a calm and steady man. In fact, as their grandfather would say, "He's a man who holds his cards close to his chest," which meant he rarely showed his emotions. That was a good thing at times like this. Both girls felt reassurance from his matter-of-fact manner.

"You know a week ago when you noticed that the Alhambra Hotel wasn't doing much business?"

Both girls nodded.

"Well," he hesitated, and then continued with great deliberateness, measuring each word, "the City Health Department had one of Mrs. Fitzsimmons' boarders taken to an isolation station for smallpox and burned his bedding."

"Smallpox!" Rachel Lee and Henrietta blurted out and then breathed in, choking on their hot chocolate.

The smallpox outbreak up north in Chicago last year remained a vivid memory in Rachel Lee's mind. The dreadful disease struck terror in everyone young and old. But she and Henrietta had a dread of all epidemics. In the 1870s, their families moved from Virginia to Cedar Glades, a mining town a few miles west of Hot Springs. It was there that Rachel Lee as a toddler, lost her parents, and Henrietta lost her mother, Uncle Samuel's his wife, in a typhoid fever epidemic.

Later, the family moved to Hot Springs. Since the girls had been too little to remember the epidemic, their grandmother, Annie MacNeil, was the only mother either of them had known.

Samuel let the news soak in for a moment. Then he cleared his voice, and continued. "Dr. Barry, you know he's the chief health official in town."

The girls nodded, affirming that they knew he worked as the city's health officer.

"He thought it best to keep it quiet as there was only one reported case, but then they discovered there were cases not reported.

"To make things worse, last Sunday the Malvern officials quarantined all the trains arriving from Hot Springs. The next day, not to be outdone, Arkadelphia quarantined against Malvern and Hot Springs. The whole story was in the *New York Times* the very next day."

"But Mr. Crane left on the train Saturday for New Orleans," Rachel Lee interrupted.

"Well, as you know the Malvern station is about 20 miles southeast of here, but at 9 miles out passengers transferred to a through train, so they wouldn't have to stop and be quarantined in Malvern," Uncle Samuel replied.

Frank Leslie's Illustrated Magazine - 1876

Courtesy of:
Hot Springs Natl. Park, AR.

"That's not much of a quarantine," Henrietta exclaimed, before sipping her hot chocolate.

The other two nodded their heads in agreement.

"Well," Samuel launched back into his story, "rumors started flying. That caused a bunch of nervous visitors to leave town as fast as they could on Monday. When they arrived in St. Louis they started telling everyone there about the outbreak, but they exaggerated conditions. Newspapers picked up the story and ran with it."

Samuel took a deep breath and continued. The girls were all ears. "That caused Dr. Barry to issue a public health report the next day, stating that the situation here was under control. Of course everyone in town realized we had a serious problem when Mrs. Fitzsimmons went before the City Council on Friday, to ask for reimbursement for the bedding destroyed by the city health department. By church time yesterday, rumors were flying again but this time there was some truth to the rumors."

Rachel Lee and Henrietta forgot all about their hot chocolate. They were transfixed by what Samuel said; their eyes never left him.

"Is that why we didn't go to church yesterday?" Henrietta questioned.

"That's right," Samuel smiled at his daughter and continued, "It seems as if the clergy all agreed to close their houses of worship for at least two weeks, probably more. The school officials have wisely followed suit.

"Unfortunately, visitors see these prudent measures as a sign that this is a really bad outbreak, and who knows, maybe they are right."

He reached down, pulled out his watch and flipped it open. "Here it is after 3 on Monday morning. And by the sound of it, we have a full-blown epidemic panic."

"How bad do you think it is?" Rachel Lee whispered the question while fearing the answer.

"Well, we have to go on what we know, and not speculate on what we don't know," her uncle stated calmly. "We've had a few infected cases that are now isolated, and two or three establishments have been quarantined.

"We also know that as early as mid-January there was a smallpox epidemic in Rody, Indiana, right on the border with Chicago. It started with the jockeys at a race track there. Then, in late January it appeared in St. Louis."

Samuel then looked from his niece, Rachel Lee, to his daughter, Henrietta, and continued. "In fact," he said, directly eyeing her, "your grandfather received a telegram from a colleague of his at Washington University in St. Louis about three weeks ago. Something about secret work on a new smallpox serum," Samuel said.

"So the news accounts from the people in St. Louis who are blaming Hot Springs for spreading the smallpox are wrong," Rachel Lee reasoned, in defense of her beloved Hot Springs.

"Not exactly," Samuel said, amused by his niece's fierce defense of her hometown. "We've done the best we could by isolating the infected and destroying anything that might have been contaminated. But that hasn't stopped other visitors infected with the disease from coming and going. Of course, it will cripple our economy if visitors stay away. What we will probably see is more cases since it takes a few days for smallpox to show up on an infected person. But our city officials are working with the federal officials on the Reservation to do what needs to be done."

The Reservation was government property that encircled the city, and most of the bath houses occupied space on the Reservation. Because the city sat right in the middle of the federal property it was very important for city and government men to work together.

"Does this mean we don't have to go to school?" Henrietta asked over her cup.

"You are not going to school; in fact there shouldn't be any public gatherings until the smallpox has been contained and suppressed," Samuel announced to the delight his daughter and niece.

"You're going to have a lot to do later this morning," Samuel continued. "But right now I want you to go back to bed and get some sleep if you can."

Samuel sat up straight and stretched his arms out wide as he yawned, "I think it's going to be a very long day for everyone."

At that moment the phone bells jingled. Everyone jumped.

"Get to bed," Samuel instructed as he stood up to answer the phone on the wall behind him.

The girls left their cups in the sink then headed toward the staircase to bed. Samuel's voice trailed after them.

"Ethan, yes come on, you can have breakfast here. Same here, it's pandemonium ... yes, all the boarders are leaving except Miss Hurley ... I'm sure you are."

Ethan Stephens was the new druggist in town. Rachel Lee and Henrietta knew he was sweet on Miss Amber.

She and Henrietta were both happy that Miss Amber planned to stay. She was so beautiful, inside and out. Everyone thought her hair looked beautiful. It appeared long and honey-colored with a natural waviness, not unruly hair like she and Henrietta's. Also, Miss Amber was the only woman Rachel Lee knew that no matter what she wore she always looked like she stepped out of the lady's fashion page. But the best thing about her was that she was never cross with anyone. All the time she had known her, Miss Amber had never appeared angry. Not once.

The girls passed through the dining room, darted up the stairs, and quickly made their way down the cold hallway. When they saw Miss Amber's light on they conspired to let her know that Mr. Stephens would soon arrive.

"Good morning girls," Miss Amber greeted. "Or should I say 'night?' " Miss Amber emerged fully dressed, her honey colored hair neatly pulled up. "Is everything alright?"

"Sure," Rachel Lee stammered. "We've been talking to Papa. We know all about the smallpox."

Rachel Lee knew they couldn't be so obvious as to blurt out what they knew about Mr. Stephens coming to the boarding house. But she had an idea. If Miss Amber sat with them at the window, she might catch a glimpse of him entering their boarding house.

"You have got to see what is happening from upstairs," Rachel Lee pleaded. Everyone in the house knew Rachel Lee's window had the best view of the neighborhood, and all the way to part of Hot Springs Mountain.

The girls' bedroom felt good and toasty by now as the three settled themselves on the window seat, cracked the window and looked out on a city in chaos. The clatter of carriages and high pitched voices drifted up from the plaza and beyond.

"I heard they are going to run special trains all day long and they are going to be adding on cars." Miss Amber offered.

"Well it sure looks like they are going to need them," Henrietta responded.

As they watched out the window at the scene below Rachel Lee suddenly thought about their friends, Henry and Jake.

Henry and Jake could have come in contact with smallpox since they both sell newspapers to visitors.

Rachel Lee decided to make a point to find them as soon as she could.

Chapter 2

Cleaning

By the time the sun reached high noon, most of the boarders had left the Annie MacNeil boarding house. Rachel Lee and Henrietta sat alone in the kitchen eating a pork sandwich. Their grandmother tended to the departing guests. The Graves, who were the last to leave had said their goodbyes to the girls, and were now loading their belongings in the carriage out by the front porch.

Rachel Lee knew her grandmother felt a deep sense of sadness to see Mrs. Emily Graves leave. They had a common bond. The bond went deeper than the common loss of family and friends that many experienced in the War Between the States. Like her grandmother said, they talked the same language, the language of common experiences that stretched back to childhood. She knew her grandmother would miss afternoon tea with Mrs. Graves and talk of the days before the war.

"Grandmother is sure sorry to see Miss Emily leave," Henrietta spoke with her mouth full. Talking with her mouth full was something she couldn't do around adults.

Rachel Lee nodded in agreement. "I was thinking the same thing."

The other guests left town before the girls awakened. Everyone else had left the house also, except their grandmother.

"Well, girls, that's that," their grandmother spoke in a soft tone as she entered the kitchen. She poured herself a cup of coffee and sat down at the table with the girls.

Rachel Lee noticed her grandmother's shoulders were pulled down as if she carried a heavy load. On impulse Rachel Lee patted her grandmother on the arm. Her grandmother gave her a half-smile and a thank you look with her dark eyes that always seemed to twinkle.

For a moment the trio sat in silence.

Suddenly, Annie sat up, straightened her shoulders, and looked each girl in the eye.

"Dr. Barry has called an emergency public health meeting. Your grandfather, Samuel, and Miss Amber went with some others to help him organize against the epidemic," Annie explained in a take-charge manner. With that, Mrs. MacNeil pulled her to-do list in front of her and picked up her pencil to write. "We're going to have to get organized as well. We have a lot to do and not much time to do it."

"This was more like it," Rachel Lee thought, "Grandmother was back in control and bringing order to the world."

"First thing I want you to do is strip your beds," their grandmother instructed. "Bundle up your bedding, dirty clothes, wash cloths, and bathing towels. Take them downstairs to the washroom. We will deal with them later. Go ahead, do it right now while I finish my list. You can take care of the dishes later."

The girls put their plates and cups in the kitchen sink and ran upstairs to get their dirty laundry.

When they came back through the kitchen with their load Annie stopped them for a moment with more instructions. "Girls, pick up a couple of buckets, some rags, and a bar of soap on your way back up."

"Okay," Rachel Lee responded.

"What are we going to wash? Henrietta inquired.

"*Everything*," Annie replied, mysteriously.

The girls re-appeared with the cleaning items their grandmother requested and found her standing by the stove.

"Bring the buckets here," she instructed, and filled the containers half-full of hot water. "Off we go," she said as she turned and headed out the kitchen through the dining room, and up the stairs with the girls in tow.

It became clear their destination was the third floor.

"We'll start with the beds," Annie commanded as they entered the girl's bedroom. "I want you girls to take your mattresses out on the side lawn. There should be sunlight over there by now. Prop them up against the retaining wall." While giving the girls instructions Anne took Henrietta's bucket and the bar of soap. "I'll have a good start by the time you get back," Annie stated. "I'll wash the bed frames, you rinse," she nodded toward Rachel Lee, "and Henrietta, you will dry. Now hurry up, I don't want any rust setting up on these springs."

Rachel Lee and Henrietta did as they were told and hurried back to help their grandmother.

Annie worked fast, and the girls did all they could to keep up.

After a few minutes, Annie spoke again. "With an epidemic in town we're going to have a lot to do. The first thing is to clean and sanitize as best we can."

The girls didn't have to be told about sanitation. They knew it ranked right up there with ventilation. They considered any house unhealthy that lacked sanitation and ventilation.

"Did any of our boarders have smallpox?" Rachel Lee asked.

"It's hard to say, since it takes days for the symptoms to appear," Annie answered.

Rachel Lee could tell from the crisp way her grandmother answered that she didn't want to speculate on what person may or may not have contracted the smallpox.

"Now, no more talk about the epidemic. We have our hands full right now getting the house sanitized," Annie stated. As she talked Annie moved over to the other side of the room and started cleaning Rachel Lee's bed. "We'll know more about the epidemic when your grandfather and Samuel get back from their meeting," Annie said.

The three worked quietly for a minute or so until Annie broke the silence. "Miss Amber is going to stop by Woodbine and help Mary and the boys pack up some of their belongings."

The girls stopped their work at this news.

"Maggie is going to have her hands full with this epidemic, so Mary and the boys are going to stay with us until it's over."

"Oh boy!" the girls exclaimed

"That's the best news I've heard all day," Henrietta stated.

"Me, too!" Rachel Lee exclaimed.

The O'Sullivans and MacNeils were like family, but Henry and Jake were also Rachel Lee and Henrietta's best friends. Jake looked small for his 9 years, but his brother Henry who was going to be 13 in a couple of weeks looked more like 14. Like Rachel Lee, he looked big for his age. His coal black wavy hair and dark blue eyes set in a finely featured face produced a striking look. Their mother, Maggie O'Sullivan, worked as an important nurse at the St. Joseph infirmary on the north end of town, way up from the government hospital and the thermal springs downtown. Mr. O'Sullivan died in a mining accident near Cedar Glades a year ago and that's when Maggie O'Sullivan and the boys moved to Woodbine Street. Mrs. O'Sullivan's sister-in-law, Mary McNulty, came to America from Ireland to help with the boys. Mary was also a good cook and did most of the cooking for the MacNeil boarding house.

After this news the girls started work with newfound vigor.

Late in the afternoon, Annie decided she and the girls could stop for the day. They had stripped and cleaned all the beds, carried the dirty sheets to the laundry room, aired and returned all mattresses, and re-made the beds.

Back in the kitchen, they sipped hot tea and nibbled on a bit of mulberry jam and toast. "I'm so thankful we have plenty of soap on hand," Annie sighed.

"What would happen if we didn't have soap?" Henrietta inquired.

"Oh, honey, I am afraid none of us would be very healthy. There are little ones all over the world who die every day from the lack of soap and water, mostly from diarrheal diseases," Annie lamented.

That was as much as either girl wanted to know about the need for soap. Their grandmother knew a lot about medicine. She could talk about diseases, cleanliness, and bodily functions all day long without much encouragement.

"Are you girls going to have enough energy to head down to Woodbine with the cart?" Annie asked.

"Yes," they said at the same time. Both girls perked up at the thought of getting out of the house.

"Alright then, I am going to need you to help Mary and the boys with their belongings."

"What about Mrs. O'Sullivan?" Rachel Lee asked as she wiped her mouth with a pale green woven cotton napkin.

"Maggie will be helping out with the smallpox cases till this epidemic is over," their grandmother explained.

Rachel Lee suddenly thought of their friend, Max, whose family owned a dairy on the edge of town. She sure hoped he didn't have the smallpox. Jake might know something since he and Max were partners in their secret business. She knew she would have to wait until they got down to Woodbine to find out anything.

The boys sold *Goodwin's Official Turf Guide* during horse racing season. The guide listed what horses ran that season. They also sold Max's racing tips. They kept the business secret because none of the grownups in their families approved of the town's gambling element.

Max knew a good horse when he saw one. He also knew all the jockeys and that fact worried Rachel Lee. Uncle Samuel said that jockeys from up north near Chicago had smallpox, and regularly visited Hot Springs racetrack this time of the year.

"I want you girls to go by way of Prospect," their grandmother instructed. "There will be fewer people to run into. If you do see anyone keep a good distance. And I want all of you back here before dark." She thought for a moment and then added, "After today we will all have to stay close to home for a while."

Chapter 3

Woodbine Street

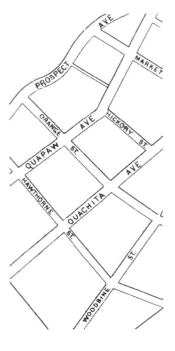

Usually Rachel Lee and Henrietta walked the zig-zag route to Henry and Jake's house. They would cut down West Lane to Quapaw Avenue, take a right and then a left down Hickory Street to Ouachita Avenue and then another right to Hawthorne Street, then another left down to Woodbine Street. But their grandmother had given them clear instructions. They were to walk Prospect Avenue straight to Hawthorne Street and down to Woodbine Street.

As the girls approached Hawthorne Street, and Henrietta prepared to turn the cart down the hill toward Quapaw Avenue, Rachel Lee noticed that the late afternoon shadow already stretched down the face of West Mountain, and had started crawling across

Prospect Avenue. She knew they would have to hurry in order to make it back home by dark. They picked up a great deal of speed heading downhill and soon flew across Quapaw and Ouachita Avenues, and turned onto Woodbine Street still breathing heavily from their run. Henry and Jake were tying down their family's cart out in the front yard. The O'Sullivan cart was much larger and it was the kind you had to pull, like you would a wagon. It had handles and a kind of harness to make the pulling easier.

"Hey, kids!" Jake greeted the girls in his usual style, leaving his older brother to finish off the tie-down.

"Hey!" the girls greeted. Henrietta parked her smaller cart between Henry and the O'Sullivan front porch.

The O'Sullivan home looked neat and well kept, surrounded by a large yard. The better part of the backyard had a garden with a white picket fence. Rachel Lee could see that Henry had already broken up the ground in preparation for planting.

"Bless ya lassie," the boy's Aunt Mary hailed a welcome, as she came out the front screen door. Mary McNulty, although a widow who had seen her share of misery, was a warm hearted soul who always filled the considerable space around her with good cheer. She carried a box of jars of preserved pears in her arms. "You made it," Mary hailed the girls.

"We hurried as fast as we could," Henrietta spoke as she ran up the front steps and took the box from Mary.

Again the front screen door flew open and Miss Amber emerged onto the front porch with another box of preserved food. "Hello girls."

"Hi Miss Amber," the girls sang in unison.

"I have one more load for the cart and we'll be on our way," Mary said. Mary turned and disappeared through the door. She moved fast even though she was a large, mature woman.

"I guess I'll be breaking up your garden pretty soon," Henry commented, nodding toward the back yard as he finished his tie-off on the cart. "Mrs. Ellsworth had me till her garden last week. I think she and Dr. Ellsworth want to have the first garden in this year. Said she was going to plant her potatoes, peas, radishes, and lettuce this week. But I think it's way too early. I'm not going to plant for another couple of weeks at least."

The Ellsworth's had wealth and lived at the other end of town on Park Avenue. Mrs. Ellsworth's brother, Mr. Van Patten, who worked as an architect, lived on Prospect Avenue.

"It does seem early," she agreed, but Rachel Lee wanted to ask about Max, not talk gardening. "I want to ask you something," she said, deliberately lowering her voice in a way that caught Henry's direct attention. "Uncle Samuel said that in January there was a smallpox epidemic at a race track up north, and that it started with the jockeys."

"I hadn't heard that," Henry said.

"I got to thinking about Max, you know, he's always talking to the jockeys."

Henry took a moment to absorb the information. "Well, he's probably okay. Mother told us that dairy people don't get smallpox as easily as other people because most of them have had the cowpox from milking. Remember those sores Max had on his hands a couple of months ago?"

"I remember," Rachel Lee said. "He did have cowpox because I saw the scars the other day. Is that the same as smallpox?"

"Well, I guess its close enough, maybe like a first cousin," Henry grinned.

"Henry, we need you to tie this down in a minute," Amber spoke in Henry's direction.

Mary came back out onto the porch followed by Mrs. O'Sullivan. Maggie O'Sullivan had red hair and red eyebrows. Rachel Lee didn't know anyone who had red eyebrows. She was also the whitest person she had ever seen. But she never looked pale. Her cheeks had a rosy color to them, what her grandmother called a "peaches and cream complexion." Rachel Lee didn't feel entirely comfortable around Mrs. O'Sullivan, not like talking with Mary. Mrs. O'Sullivan always acted stern, like you better mind your P's and Q's … or else.

"Girls, you be sure and tell your grandmother I said hello," Mrs. O'Sullivan said.

"We will," the girls promised.

"Jake, Henry, it's going to be dark soon. You had best get going," Mrs. O'Sullivan directed.

Rachel Lee could tell that Mrs. O'Sullivan didn't give to hugging, not even her own boys. "That was the way it was with some people," Rachel Lee thought to herself. "They didn't love any less," she guessed, "it was just that some people let the harshness in their life take all the tenderness out of them." She resolved that this wouldn't ever happen to her. She wanted to be like her grandmother. No one in the world could hug any better than her grandmother. She knew no matter what happened anywhere in the world, when her grandmother hugged her nothing bad would ever happen to her.

All of a sudden Rachel Lee felt a long way from home and wanted to get back as soon as possible. Without having to be told, she bid Mrs. O'Sullivan goodbye and turned her cart for home. Everyone else said their goodbyes and took up the road behind her.

By the time they crossed Ouachita Avenue dusk had set in. The closer they came to Prospect Avenue the steeper Hawthorne Street got. This caused Rachel Lee to slow down considerably. Henry came up alongside of her puffing, and when they were even he turned toward Jake and Henrietta, and barked out an order for them to help push. They crossed Quapaw Avenue and made the final push up the hill to

Prospect Avenue. By then everyone was breathing very hard.

"Whooo! That was a climb-and-a-half," Henry let out as he sat the front end of the cart down, turned loose of the handles and sat down on the cart's front edge. Rachel Lee sat on one of the handles of her cart and the others leaned on Henry's cart.

"Oh, I got to catch me breath," Mary wheezed.

After a minute more everyone agreed to get going. They still had two blocks to go and darkness had started on Prospect Avenue, next to the mountain.

Rachel Lee didn't relax till they rounded the bend in the road and saw her own front porch. Through the darkness she saw the swing stop and knew her grandmother had started to walk toward them.

"Land sakes, I was beginning to worry," Mrs. MacNeil spoke as she approached them. "What a motley group you are."

"You should have seen us huffing and puffing it up Hawthorne Street. Now that was a sight," Henry responded. Henry's comment struck his fellow travelers as funny, and with what little breath they had in them they all had a fit of uncontrollable giggles. For hours they had all been scared out of their wits with talk of the smallpox epidemic, now after a long hard day all they wanted to do was laugh.

Annie laughed, too.

Rachel Lee loved to hear her grandmother laugh. She knew that her grandmother more than most understood the need to laugh in the mist of fear and panic. After all, Rachel Lee's grandparents had lived through the War Between the States and the hard years that continued under Reconstruction. They knew from that tragic experience that epidemics, like wars, caused fear and loss of life. It also scarred some and left many to beg. Poverty, the lasting legacy of every war and epidemic was the enemy they would all have to fight when the smallpox outbreak ended. Rachel Lee knew her grandmother's thoughts on wars and epidemics.

Still laughing, they shouldered their burden for the final push home. It took what little energy they all had left to unload the carts, eat supper, and get ready for bed.

Rachel Lee and Henrietta didn't have to be told twice to go to bed. As Rachel Lee trudged up the steps behind her cousin she thought of what their Grandfather said in times like this: "I'm so tired, I'm breathing from memory."

Chapter 4

The Laundry

Annie MacNeil's boarding house sat on the corner of Market Street and Prospect Avenue, at the foot of West Mountain. Like all the other boarding houses in town the usual routines had stopped. Visitors left town as fast as they could before a stronger quarantine came into effect. This left the townspeople to wash and sterilize bedding and towels, and to scrub down guest rooms.

As tired as Rachel Lee and Henrietta had been the night before, there was still too much excitement in the air to sleep in.

"Let's go see where the boys are. I'll bet they're not sleeping," Henrietta suggested in a low voice. She sat on the side of the bed putting on her shoes.

"Good idea," Rachel Lee said, and rolled out of bed and quickly got dressed.

They quietly tiptoed past Miss Amber's room to the end of the hall, where the Graves had stayed. Looking through the open door the room appeared empty.

"I knew they would be up," Henrietta whispered.

Rachel Lee placed her forefinger to her lips and pointed across the hall to Mary's room.

Beyond the boys' room there was a landing and a long stairway to the left leading down to the first floor. On the opposite side of the landing another short, but wider, staircase curved to the right leading to a larger landing and two doors. The door on the right led to their grandparents' room. It was closed. The door on the left, which led to the family library and study, was open. Boarders could borrow the books, but only family members and close friends could occupy the room. Through the library on the far side of the room, another door led to Samuel's quarters.

The girls quietly hurried down the stairs to the first floor hallway and took a left-hand turn away from the foyer and family parlor. So far they hadn't run into anyone. They passed through the dining room on the left and entered the kitchen—still no boys.

"They must be outside," Henrietta observed in a voice a little higher than a whisper.

Since health-seekers customarily rested after their morning bath treatments, the girls were used to being quiet at certain times when there wasn't school and the town was running as usual. Their grandparents also rested for a few hours after the mid-day meal because their work continued long after the girls had gone to bed.

Rachel Lee agreed they should check outside for the boys. As they passed by the kitchen stove Rachel Lee noticed that someone already had set a fire. Most mornings that was her job. She also took note of the fresh coffee. The girls now felt free to move and talk normally or at least the quiet end of normal, and ran for the back porch.

They viewed the driveway leading off Market Street to the carriage house, and then scanned the rest of the backyard and the small orchard set back to the left. Between the orchard and the backyard lay a garden ready to awaken from a long winter's nap.

The MacNeil carriage house faced the back porch. It stored everything in it but a carriage. Like most people in the neighborhood, they didn't own private transportation. The Market Street plaza community had every kind of business and retail store within walking distance. On those occasions when you needed transportation, people rode the Hot Springs public streetcar lines that ran on either side of Market Street plaza. The livery stables had horses for longer distances. The trains a little further away brought visitors to Hot Springs from all over the United States, Mexico and Canada.

"I'll bet they're around back," Rachel Lee asserted as she leaped down the stairs two at a time followed by her shorter cousin who kept to the usual one step at a time.

A clothesline stretched across a corner of the north side of the house, surrounded on two sides by a green privet hedge. A retaining wall ran along the west side and connected to the foundation of the house. The basement door and three windows faced the side yard.

The smaller one on the far left opened to the coal room and the other two, to the basement washroom.

The girls heard Henry and Jake before they saw them.

"Ouch!" Jake yelled.

That was the end of Henry's pitching practice with Jake. He found it difficult to keep a pitching partner long, since he could burn them into a glove better than anyone his age. The boys played in the space between the clothesline and the basement door. Both of them had dressed for the day, but Jake as usual had a shirttail hanging out and locks in need of a combing.

Buttercup, the family dog of Spaniel and Shepherd mix, lay under the clothesline watching the boys until he spotted Rachel Lee and Henrietta. Buttercup quickly walked over to the girls, and Henrietta wrapped her left arm around the dog's fluffy neck like it was a giant pillow. Buttercup's tail energetically wagged back and forth. He was thrilled to have so much company on a school day.

"Man, I'm glad you're here," Jake bellowed out and tossed Rachel Lee his glove, "my hand is worn out."

"Next**,**" Henry beamed. Henry took pride in wearing out catchers and Rachel Lee took pride in lasting longer than any of his other catchers.

"How about marbles?" Jake asked Henrietta while pulling out a small stringed pouch from his pocket.

"Sure."

For about a half-hour everyone in the side yard pursued a good time. Then Mary called them for breakfast. They all ran for the kitchen.

"Let's leave the marbles where they are," Jake suggested.

"Yeah, we'll come back after breakfast," Henrietta agreed as she raced behind the others.

Buttercup the family dog ran with the group to the back porch.

"Oh no! I forgot to feed Buttercup," Rachel Lee moaned.

While the others ran inside, Rachel Lee stopped at the icebox on the back porch and got leftovers from the night before. "Come on, boy," Rachel Lee spoke softly, encouraging her friend to follow her lead. Together they ran out to Buttercup's dish next to the woodbin. Most of the time Rachel Lee cleaned Buttercup's bowl first, but today she was in too big of a hurry.

When she entered the kitchen she saw her grandmother seated at the head of the table addressing the boys.

"We've all decided," Annie said while looking directly at Henry, "that it will be best if you, Jake and Mary stay with us for at least the next four weeks until the epidemic has run its course. Your mother will be terribly busy and won't be able to be home anyway. It will be more pleasant for all of us to be together. And it will be easier for all of you to keep up with your lessons."

"I thought we weren't going to have school?" Henrietta grumbled, as she and Rachel Lee served themselves breakfast.

"School is going to be closed for the next three or four weeks, but that is too long a time to go without your lessons," Mary stated from the kitchen sink.

"Miss Amber has volunteered to help out with your history and literature lessons," Annie explained. "I'll conduct spelling, math and art lessons. Each of your teachers has sent broad lesson plan outlines. Since your books are at school you won't be getting complete lessons, but we will make up for it by improvising."

Rachel Lee knew that if anyone could improvise school lessons, it would be her grandmother. She knew more words than anyone and she could turn any situation into a lesson.

"As you know, all our boarders have left except Miss Amber. So the first thing we have to do after breakfast is the laundry," their grandmother began her instructions. "Until this epidemic is over most of the establishments will probably be washing their own laundry."

Rachel Lee noticed the sense of urgency in her grandmother's voice. Like her grandmother, Rachel Lee knew the importance of the laundry business to a town like Hot Springs. Bathing prevailed as the city's main industry and brought hundreds of new people every week. The bathhouses, hotels, boarding houses, and other rooming establishments all needed clean and sanitized bedding and towels on a constant basis. The town had several laundry establishments and many individual laundresses, but as Rachel Lee began to learn, no one did business as usual during a smallpox epidemic.

"Where's Grandfather and Uncle Samuel?" She asked her Grandmother.

"They've already left …," Annie responded, then started to say more but stopped as if she couldn't think what to say next. She resumed talking with very measured words and a solemn voice. "The health department has decided to institute a city-wide vaccination against the smallpox," she said.

Not even the thought of a holiday from school could detract a person from the prospect of a smallpox vaccination. Rachel Lee had read about the vaccination, and it didn't sound like something she wanted to experience.

"Are we going to have to get vaccinated?" Henrietta asked, already knowing the answer.

"I'm afraid so. We all are," her grandmother pronounced, then added, "but it is a lot better than getting the smallpox." She continued in a half-hearted attempt to lighten the gravity of the situation. "I would sure hate to see you girls with small pox scars all over your pretty faces."

Before the children had time to dwell on the prospect of a vaccination, Annie quickly assigned everyone a particular task. "Girls, when you finish eating I have something important for you to do so let's hurry up. Henry, it will be a while before any more wood is delivered so we're going to need you to take some of the fireplace wood and chop it up for both the kitchen and laundry stoves. We're going to need lots of hot water. You know where we keep the ax?"

Henry, still chewing on a big bite of biscuit, nodded that he understood. "I'm on my way," he stated, going through the back door.

Henry always finished eating before anyone else got a good start.

Annie then addressed Rachel Lee, "Honey, when you're through eating, I need you to get the downstairs stove fired up and put the big kettle on it."

"I need to get my marbles," Jake announced before anyone could give him orders.

"Then go pick them up after you finish eating," Annie said, smiling. Turning to Henrietta she said, "Sweetie, your job will be to fill the kettle. When you get through, I want you all right back here in the kitchen."

Rachel Lee felt happy she hadn't finished eating by the time Miss Amber came into the kitchen. She wanted to find out what had happened with the epidemic.

"Oh, I can't believe it is morning already," Miss Amber announced on entering the kitchen.

"Here, take my place," Annie offered. "I'll get you some coffee."

Miss Amber gratefully sank down in the chair. "Oh, thank you," she said.

Henrietta was curious, too. "What happened last night?"

"Girls," their grandmother interrupted, "we'll take this up later. Right now you need to get moving."

Chapter 5

Soap Art

Soap art re-creation by:
Columbia Percefull & Sophie Rudder

Henry stayed outside to chop wood, but the rest of the kids returned to the kitchen to find the three women sitting at the table. Amber ate her breakfast while Mary and Annie shaved soap into hot water for the laundry.

Annie spoke first. "I've decided we're going to do an art lesson. We have to shave all this soap anyway, might as well make a lesson out of it."

"Oh, boy!" Henrietta exclaimed. She was the artist in the family so it was more like something fun to do than work.

"Grab a bar and get a paring knife from the drawer," Annie instructed. "What I want you to do is sculpt the bar into the shape of an animal. We can use the chips for the laundry."

Henrietta jumped into action right away. "I am going to make a rabbit," she said.

The other two started with less enthusiasm.

"I think I will make a fish," Jake offered. "It's the only thing I can think of to make that might look right."

Rachel Lee thought on it for a bit, knowing she couldn't draw much more than stick people and trees. Then she had an idea. "Here goes," she announced. "I'm going to let everyone guess what mine is." She thought to herself that she would sculpt a bird, but it was best not to reveal her intentions in case her effort didn't pan out.

About an hour later Henry came through the back door. He had sweat on his brow, and wet hair at the temples and at the back of his neck around his collar.

"I need to take a break," Henry gasped, breathing heavy from his labor. As he spoke he picked up his designated drinking cup and went over to the kitchen sink to get some water. He then sat down at the table across from Rachel Lee. "What is it?" he asked, looking at her work in progress.

"She wants us all to guess … mine's a fish," Jake said as he proudly held up his soap art for all to see, then began waving it up and down.

Henry grinned and said to Rachel Lee, "Good thinking."

Rachel Lee didn't respond.

"Jake, you've done a very good job. It looks good enough to eat," Henry observed.

"Thanks." He sat up a little straighter and continued waving his creation in the air.

"And I think it's a nice looking duck," her grandmother offered to Rachel Lee.

"Well, technically a duck is a bird," she thought, and then responded, "thank you."

Henrietta also had finished with her sculpted piece that looked like a rabbit, but as with most artists she was never satisfied with her composition and continued to work toward perfection.

"I need to call time on the art lesson," Annie MacNeil addressed her pupils. "Everybody scrape up your chips and put them in one of these bowls of hot water. And leave your artwork on the table. Your grandfather and Samuel will want to see them."

After the soap chips melted in the hot water everyone headed down to the basement to do the laundry.

Once the women began the washing process, the kids started their assigned readings. They seated themselves on the floor outside the wash room in front of the basement door.

After a few minutes Mary checked in on the students. "Henry," she instructed, "as soon as you get to a stopping place we're going to need you to bleed off some hot water from the boiler. We'll use it for rinsing … be that much less water for us to heat."

Henry looked up from his adventure story only long enough to answer, "Okay."

The rest of them had to read history. Jake read about the War of 1812, Rachel Lee and Henrietta read about Napoleon and his wars. Rachel Lee couldn't understand why they had to learn about Napoleon and all his wars, but since they were going to have to write an essay about him she continued reading.

They spent the rest of the day alternating between hanging laundry, lessons, and folding. By late afternoon, the students all sat around the dining room table. Henry wrote a review of his adventure novel and the rest

of them wrote essays for their reading assignment.

The ringing of the telephone bells in the kitchen broke their concentration. Rachel Lee knew her grandmother had answered the phone but couldn't make out what she said. It wasn't polite to eavesdrop, but sometimes that was the only way she and Henrietta knew what happened around the place. She wasn't the only one listening while pretending to do their homework. They all knew that when Uncle Samuel and grandfather got home they would probably all get their smallpox inoculation.

Without warning, Annie entered the dining room. The kids jumped.

"That was your grandfather," Annie said to the girls before she sat at the head of the table to address everyone. "That will be enough lessons for now. I need you to bring in the sheets off the line and put them away. Then get cleaned up for supper. We'll have to eat without the men tonight."

"Why?" Rachel Lee blurted out.

"Well, a city-wide inoculation is an enormous undertaking. And they are going to clean up and change clothes before they come home. They're at the other end of town right now, at Mr. Rockafellow's bathhouse. He's letting the public health workers clean up at his place before they go home."

That made sense to the kids.

"After supper we are all going to get to bed early," Annie instructed her young charges.

No one argued as they all felt tired. It had been another full day for everyone.

Chapter 6

The Inoculation

Wednesday morning was well underway by the time the girls awakened. They might have stayed asleep if not for the departing train's unusually long blow of its whistle. They hurriedly dressed and made their way down from the tower room, scurrying along the hallway where boarders normally resided. They sensed the emptiness of the upstairs floor. As they descended to the first floor they heard familiar voices from the kitchen and smelled the aroma of freshly fried bacon.

The girls' grandfather, Doctor Robert MacNeil, and their grandmother sat at the table with their backs turned. Dr. MacNeil stood tall and while not portly, the years had added to his girth as it had to Annie's, who was large boned and tall like Rachel Lee. Only the back of their heads could be seen. While grey had begun to replace their naturally dark hair, they both retained a semblance of their original dark brown. Henry sat between them.

A large linen cloth covered their grandparents' end of the table. Dr. MacNeil's medical bag and medicine case sat prominently on the table to his left. He had neatly arranged his inoculation tools in front of him.

"Good morning, girls," their grandmother said, as she turned her head in their direction while holding fast to Henry's arm. The girls saw their grandfather concentrate on vaccinating Henry.

"Mornin' lassies," Mary McNulty greeted them from the kitchen stove. "Tis a fine sleep ye've had and I think ye needed it."

"Hey kids," Jake greeted them from the far end of the kitchen table. He sat comfortably in his usual ill-fitting hand-me-downs from his old brother, waiting his turn to be vaccinated. His chestnut hair appeared neatly combed, an uncharacteristic state for him.

The girls stood by the door, barely in the kitchen, with the water pump and sink to their immediate right.

"It's no big deal," Henry interjected.

Rachel Lee knew Henry had seen the distressed look on their faces and tried to assure them.

"Henry's right," their grandfather spoke in calm agreement. "I place a drop of the vaccine onto the skin then take this special instrument called a point and gently scrape across the skin a few times."

"Alright Jake, you're next," Dr. MacNeil spoke with a no-nonsense air of authority. Henry stood up at the same moment. And the girls jumped back in an instinctive reflex. Too late, though; once they entered the kitchen, there was no escape.

Rachel Lee felt terrified of smallpox. Wild thoughts ran through her head. What if something went wrong with the inoculation, she wondered, and she got a bad case of it? Even if she didn't die, she would be horribly scarred for life; her face all pockmarked like some of the visitors she had seen.

Mary set her cooking aside to ready the girls for their vaccination. "Roll up your left sleeve," she addressed both girls. "We need to wash your upper arm." Mary steered the two girls toward the kitchen sink, picked up a clean washcloth and a bar of soap, and began to scrub Henrietta's arm.

Rachel Lee knew the smell. Yesterday, the whole basement smelled like soap. Familiar smells were good; they were part of what was normal. And Rachel Lee sure needed some normal right now. Many of the visitors to Hot Springs smelled of the same soap her grandmother used because it felt gentle to the skin. Hospitals also recommended it and only this brand floated. These were all good reasons for her grandmother to use it. That was Rachel Lee's thoughts on the regular soap her family used.

The girls turned to watch Jake get his vaccination. Rachel Lee couldn't see Jake's face as her grandfather began the inoculation process, but she had a clear view of her friend's arm. First her grandfather placed a small drop of vaccine on his upper arm, then took the point, held it in his hand like a pencil, and carefully scraped across the drop several times. She took note of the fact that Jake didn't flinch and that put her more at ease.

"Darlin', I need your arm," Mary said, as she put her hand on Rachel Lee's shoulder to turn her around. Henrietta stood close by, patting her arm dry.

Their grandmother took Jake aside and blotted the inoculated arm with a small piece of cotton cloth. Meanwhile, their grandfather prepared to deliver another vaccination. Rachel Lee and Henrietta stood by and waited their fate. Henrietta received her inoculation first while Mary rinsed off Rachel Lee's arm. Their grandparents' strategy worked: vaccinate quickly before anyone had time to balk.

"Go ahead and have a seat," Annie directed Jake, as she placed the cotton cloth in a waste container for later burning. "You will have to wait a few minutes till the area is absolutely dry before you roll your sleeve down."

When the process ended, Dr. MacNeil cleared the table of all the medical equipment. "I'll tend to the burning," he stated as he picked up the waste container and left the room. Rachel Lee thought he looked awfully tired.

Annie proceeded to wash down the table. Mary went back to cooking. No one spoke a word until Annie wiped the table. "Now, that's done," she proclaimed, and without another word joined Mary in getting breakfast ready.

An air of deep seriousness pervaded the kitchen. Rachel Lee and the others stayed silent, each lost in their own thoughts.

The women served breakfast in silence. The family had half-eaten the meal by the time Dr. MacNeil re-entered the kitchen several minutes later. He carried a typewritten document. Rachel Lee could see he still had a very serious expression, almost a frown, something she hardly ever saw on her grandfather.

Henry, Henrietta, and Rachel Lee all sat on the bench with their backs to the windows, facing the kitchen stove. Jake sat on the bench at the end of the table.

Dr. MacNeil took a deep breath, sat down at the head of the table, and addressed the children. "I need to have a serious talk with everyone," placing a document on the kitchen table to his left as he spoke. He waited until Mary and Annie set the cooking aside, once again, and joined the others at the table.

Looking straight at the children he announced, "This is not going to give you smallpox."

Rachel Lee knew her grandfather had seen the terrified look on their faces. She repeated her grandfather's words in her head, "This is not going to give you smallpox." Then she counted the words: eight of the most beautiful words she had ever heard. She almost laughed at herself. "Why did I count the words?" she wondered.

"I am going to tell you exactly what is going to happen," her grandfather continued. "The more we know about a scary situation, the less we're apt to be frightened by it. In three or four days a small reddish, raised area will appear at your inoculation site. It may itch and it may remain sore, but do not scratch or rub this area. For the next week it will continue to grow and fill up with fluid. It is extremely important to let someone know if any fluid from your vaccinated area escapes this stage. That way we can avoid any complications. In about a week from now it will start draining. It will dry up and form a scab. Sometime during the third or fourth week the scab will fall off. And you will be left with a small scar on your shoulder. Everyone have a clear picture of this?"

Four heads nodded in unison.

"I'm going to need to check your vaccinated area in three days, then again in six and once more in nine days, to make sure the vaccine took and everything looks alright. One thing more, no one ... I mean no one is to share a towel, washcloth, or any other personal item until the vaccination area has healed.

"Is this perfectly understood?"

Again four heads nodded in unison.

"Good."

He then slid the typewritten document in front of their grandmother. "Annie, I'll be out of touch for the next few hours. We've had word that a storm and heavy rain is headed our way for later this evening. Let's hope it holds off until evening. Here is a copy of the vaccination schedule. Samuel and Miss Hurley are already hard at it."

He waited a moment, giving her time to look over the schedule.

"As you can see the health board has assigned me to the Quapaw/Prospect area from Violet Street to Grand Avenue. Most of the drugstores already have ample vaccination supplies since they arrived here yesterday from the through train to St. Louis. Also,

Martin Eisele and the Harrell brothers have contacts that will ship any more supplies the board might need."

"I don't want you over-doing," Annie stated as she placed a hand on her husband's arm.

He smiled. It was the first smile the children had seen on his face in days.

Rachel Lee felt relieved to see her grandfather smile, and both her grandparents' customary affection toward one another. This, too, was normal.

"Samuel and Miss Amber promised to return by 6 o'clock for supper. I want you back here by then also," Annie said.

At the second mention of Miss Amber, Rachel Lee and Henrietta forgot all about smallpox, and made a familiar face at one another as they simultaneously scrunched up their shoulders. It was a silent communication, practiced by young people the world over, especially those engaged in ongoing intrigues that involved the adults in their lives.

"One more thing before I go," Dr. MacNeil announced to everyone. "The City Council is going to meet tomorrow and institute quarantine measures. From now on, no one is to leave the property."

Everyone nodded that they understood.

After Dr. MacNeil departed, Mary started washing the dirty pots and pans since she and Annie had already eaten. Annie continued with instructions for the day while the young people finished eating.

"Jake, when you have finished eating," Annie MacNeil directed, "I want you and Henrietta to go to the linen closet and get the towels and washcloths that have the embroidered initials on them. I've put everyone's initials on two washcloths and two towels for each of us. Separate them out and take them to everyone's room. When you are through I want you to get the slate boards and come back down to the dining room."

"The slate boards," Henrietta stated.

"Yes, we are going to do a math lesson later on. But we have a more important project to do at the moment."

Annie then addressed her other granddaughter, "Honey, I'll need you to go to the linen closet also and take the step stool with you. On the top shelf there is a big box of old muslin sheets." At this point Annie reached into the pocket of her apron and retrieved a piece of muslin the size used to dab the vaccine drop after inoculation. "Bring it down to the dining room," Annie instructed her granddaughter. "I've put three on the dining room table. When you two are through separating the linen I want you to help Rachel Lee and Henry cut squares exactly like this one.

"Why do we need so many pieces of cloth this size?" Henrietta asked before anyone else could.

"Well, it's going to be our contribution to the city-wide vaccination. I'll need you to bring them here to the kitchen and put them in the boiling water that Mary is preparing. After they are good and sterilized we'll carefully dry and package them." Annie answered, adding, "Everyone must help out because the Health Committee will need a lot of sterile wipes."

"Oh, I see," Henrietta responded. At the same time the others nodded that they also understood. "Is everyone in the whole town going to be vaccinated?" she questioned.

Annie addressed Rachel Lee's question with amusement, "Everyone they find. Some people are dead set against the vaccination and are trying to hide out. But Dr. Barry and the other men assigned to help with the inoculation are determined men, including your grandfather."

Her answer satisfied everyone and as they started to troop out of the kitchen she made a parting announcement. "After you finish cutting the pieces we'll do our math lesson," Annie concluded.

Chapter 7

The End of Quarantine

Jake and Rachel Lee sat with their backs to the retaining wall in the side yard while their euchre partners sat directly across from them. Everyone looked intently at the cards in their hands.

"Jack!" Henry exclaimed, showing his jack of hearts.

"Oh, Pooh," Henrietta sighed.

"Nine days we've been playing this silly card game. I'm sick of it," Jake said before throwing down his cards. "I'll be glad when tomorrow comes."

Everyone else agreed, including Henry who played the game better than anyone else.

For nine days while the smallpox vaccination ran its course, everyone at the MacNeil Boarding house fell into a routine of morning chores, then lessons, followed by playtime until dinner. Playtime soon turned into routine playtime which was not as enjoyable as plain old playing around. All of their activity fell within the boundaries of the MacNeil property, except for Buttercup's daily walk by himself up West Mountain.

After a week-and-a-half everyone became restless, especially so today because they had been told this morning that since they had not had any complications with their vaccinations, they could go back to school which would re-open Monday.

"Even working in the garden is a welcome break," Rachel Lee commented as she gathered up everyone's cards.

"Right now, even school looks good," Henrietta added.

Before anyone else could respond they heard Mary calling them to dinner.

They didn't have to be called twice. Each one scrambled trying to arrive first at the back steps. Inside, everyone took turns washing hands at the kitchen sink and then made their way into the dining room. They were half-way through eating before Dr. MacNeil, Samuel, Ethan, and Miss Amber arrived back at the boarding house.

"We're going back to school Monday," Henrietta blurted out in her father's direction.

"Yes, I've heard," he smiled, "can't believe you are excited about going back to school."

"Me, neither," Henrietta confessed with a grin.

Rachel Lee noticed as her grandfather sat down that he looked tired like all the grownups looked since the smallpox epidemic started. His shoulders appeared more weighed down this week than ever before. He had extra reason for fatigue. He had an assignment to check all the people he vaccinated on a schedule of three times in the past nine days. He performed the assignment on top of seeing regular patients at his practice. But now that it looked like all his vaccinations worked, he didn't look as worried as he had the past few days. Rachel Lee felt happy that he had fewer worries.

"Since you are going home tomorrow," Annie announced, looking down the table at Henry, Mary and Jake, "I think we will have some fun tonight." Then she directed her attention to Rachel Lee and Henrietta as well. "After dinner I want all of you to get into your bed clothes and go to the library. We're going to pop some popcorn and maybe get Mary to tell us a story."

Everyone enjoyed Mary's stories, even the adults, and everybody liked popcorn. It didn't take Rachel Lee and the other kids long to change into bed clothes and scamper toward the library. Rachel Lee and Henrietta bounced from the hallway and up the stairs to the next landing. They found the boys in the library with Samuel.

"Wait a minute," Rachel Lee exclaimed in mid-air, turned and nearly knocked Henrietta off the landing. "I'll get the popcorn and popper."

"Don't forget the bowls," Henrietta said, as she righted herself on the landing.

Soon after Rachel Lee returned, the powerful aroma of popcorn replaced the usual scent of leather that filled the library. Everyone had a turn at shaking the long-handled popper over the fireplace flames.

After cleaning his pipe Samuel stretched out in the Morris chair. The chair had arms and a lower frame of quarter-sawn oak. The seat, back and pull-out footrest exhibited shiny dark bronze-colored leather. Moss green and rosy pink tapestry-covered pillows rested at his back. Dr. MacNeil sat at his desk finishing up his smallpox report for the City Health Committee.

"How about starting some for me," Samuel nodded toward Henry as he began filling his pipe.

"Sure thing," Henry replied.

"Grandfather, you want me to make some for you?" Rachel Lee asked.

"Please, I'll be through with this in a minute, and then I finally will be able to relax," Dr. MacNeil sighed.

Annie and Mary joined the others about the time Henry finished with Samuel's popcorn.

"Take mine," Samuel offered his mother and Mary. "Here I'll do this batch."

Rachel Lee gladly handed over the popper and joined her cousin and friends on the couch opposite her grandmother and Aunt Mary.

This was Mary's cue to take command of the room. "Everyone settled?" Mary asked.

Heads nodded.

"Once upon a time … a long, long time ago …" Mary always started her stories the same way. No one knew exactly how long, long ago was, but everyone knew that the best stories happened a long time ago.

"… high on a hill, there stood a proud old wooden house. It had gables and gingerbread patterns and a wide front porch that curved around each side.

Children played on the steps and older people rocked in the swing or rockers. T'was a fine, good family.

The front door had a magnificent stained glass face and halfway down the door on the left hand side was Little Dimple Doorknob. Oh, but he was a bright and shiny brass knob, and such a joy to look upon."

Mary began to get more and more animated.

Dr. MacNeil had finished his report and now sat in a side chair close to Annie.

"His face gleamed with a finely polished sparkle. The craftsman who made him molded a fine design with curlicues and dimples. His dimples, of course, were his finest features.

Dimple loved being part of this fine old house, and the fine old house loved him, from the gables on the top to the railing on the porch.

For many years, Little Dimple Doorknob stood watch at the entrance to this fine old house. Then one cold December dawn, the house woke to the crackling sound of burning timbers," Mary spoke in terrified tones.

"The family and their cat and dog ran from the burning house. Little Dimple Doorknob could hear the fire wagon racing up the hill, but it was too late. The house was all in flames, the front door became unhinged and had fallen.

Little Dimple Doorknob lay with his face turned up. A beam lay across his curlicues and dimples. His face was charred and sooty black; all the bright and shiny of him gone.

For weeks, he lay in the ruins of this once fine old house till one day there came the sound of hammers and saws.

Dimple was roughly torn from the burned front door and thrown in a box with the other damaged house fixtures. It was suffocating to be in such a crowded box.

Days passed and still he traveled in this crowded, stinky old box, handed from one person to the next.

Finally," Mary exclaimed, "an old man took him from the box, washed him off a little and placed him on a shelf with other worn out and scarred up doorknobs.

Day-in and day-out poor Little Dimple sat on the shelf. Every day some man or woman would pick him up, look him over and put him back on the shelf. Dimple knew if the old man would clean and shine him up someone would come to give him a home.

One day the old man placed him in a box again with all the other knobs."

"Not again," Henrietta blurted out.

"Yes," Mary continued, "and they traveled to a faraway place where a lot of people had gathered. And when they got there the old man emptied his boxes on a long table. Dimple had not seen the sun in a very long time. It felt so warm. Soon, a part of his old gleam caught a ray of the sun.

All morning long he was handled and passed around till sometime around about the middle of the day a young man decided to pick up Little Dimple Doorknob.

He was placed in a sack and taken from the crowd of people. Dimple's heart beat with excitement knowing he may soon have a new home. But after two days he began to worry. Then at last the young man took him from the sack and cleaned and polished Dimple's face. At long last he looked like himself again. For hours the young man shined and buffed, shined and buffed. Little Dimple Doorknob never looked so good.

When the young man was finished he attached Dimple to the front door of his house. Then he showed his handiwork to his wife and daughter who squealed with delight. This not only made the young man happy, but made Dimple feel very proud.

Neither the door nor the house was quite as magnificent as the old house, but Dimple did not mind. He had a new home and a new family and that was all that really mattered.

"Oh, Mary, that's so sweet," Annie exclaimed. "What an imagination you have!"

Everyone else smiled in agreement.

For a few minutes in the upstairs library, Rachel Lee and everyone else at Annie MacNeil's Boarding house had forgotten the smallpox epidemic and the hard times it left in its wake.

Chapter 8

Reservation Piglet

Returning to school was not as fun as Rachel Lee and Henrietta had thought it would be. Most students, including many of their friends, stayed home even though everyone knew the schools had re-opened a week ago.

Some had complications from their vaccination, but most stayed away because they were too scared to attend. The fear of smallpox gripped the whole town even though everyone had been vaccinated.

Rachel Lee felt so thankful that no one she knew had scars from the smallpox, except from the vaccination.

This being a Saturday morning usually meant market day, when people came into town from the surrounding farms to buy and sell. That didn't happen this day. And, of course, visitors stayed away. People feared the smallpox.

Neighbors talked of business failures and how they would have to scratch around to find money to live on until next spring.

"Are you sure you don't see anything?" Henry asked.

"Yes, I am sure," Jake replied, irritated at his older brother's impatience.

The two cousins, two brothers and their friend, Max, all sat nestled securely in a group of oaks on the northeast slope of Hot Springs Mountain. They had chosen the trees close to the pig trail, and they all sat in limbs close to the ground. Max and Jake sat in a tree east of Henry. Rachel Lee hugged a limb in the next tree to the north of Henry, and Henrietta stayed perched some distance west of everyone else.

Rachel Lee loved to climb trees! Like all good tree climbers, she had her favorite trees. The tree in which she sat didn't rank on her list of favorites. The limbs angled sharply upwards. She had little room between the trunk and branch to sit in comfort. But she didn't mind the discomfort as she and the others began their adventure to capture a piglet whose mother was wild. The adults called the mother pig feral, meaning a wild pig. Humans probably raised her, but the pig later escaped into the forest that covered the mountains on the Reservation and she became feral.

The idea to capture one of the piglets hit Rachel Lee and Henry at the same time. Henry had told them about the mother pig and her babies a week before the epidemic. Henry had helped Mrs. Ellsworth with her garden and had noticed the mother pig foraging on the other side of the Ellsworth fence. He could tell she had a litter to nurse.

Later, when Rachel Lee and Henrietta read about the French during Napoleon's time they learned about certain French foods like Roquefort cheese, truffles and escargot. They thought it funny that adults used pigs to find truffles.

The delicacies sounded exotic until their grandmother explained escargot as a French word for snails and that truffles, while very expensive, grew as fungus in the ground that people dug up like a potato. In fact, truffles looked a lot like ugly misshaped potatoes.

Their grandmother had had an idea for the children to spend some time in the family library studying about fungus. She knew many types of fungus grew in certain areas of their region of the country, the Ouachita springs region. When she mentioned that summer truffles grew on the family's property near Cedar Glades and some of the other open woodlands in the area, the idea of training one of the feral piglets to harvest truffles hit Henry and Rachel Lee at the same time.

Their grandfather became delighted over their interest in the branch of science that concerned fungi called mycology. But his delight came more from a scientific point of view rather than commercial.

"This summer's visit to Cedar Glades is going to be so beneficial to everyone's education," their grandfather said. But their grandmother had added with a wink at the children that it would be fun, too.

At the moment, Rachel Lee and Henry didn't care about science or fun. They wanted to make money to help their families.

Later, when Annie quizzed them on what they had learned, they discussed the subject of a market for summer truffles. They talked about summer truffles as less potent in taste and aroma than the winter truffle but perfect for light summer dishes.

Her grandmother agreed that there was a good market for summer truffles in St. Louis, Memphis, and New Orleans. She also commended them on their business sense adding, "Education is a good thing, but education alone doesn't put food on the table."

Annie enthusiastically supported their plans to capture and train a pig for truffle harvesting, but told them they had to get permission from Superintendent William Little since the Reservation was government property. Mr. Little didn't mind. He said they were helping the government by helping to thin out the feral pig population.

"I see them coming," Jake announced in a loud whisper through cupped hands in Henry's direction.

"Get ready," Henry whispered back, then quickly turned to Rachel Lee, "Get ready."

Everyone held their breath as the mother pig and her six half-grown piglets made their way down the trail toward the residential neighborhood where the Ellsworth's lived. They had passed Jake and Max and now approached Henry's perch. They had a simple plan. Henry would create a diversion by jumping down to grab one of the piglets. He would run back to Jake and Max who held a burlap blanket, ready to receive the squealing piglet before leaping up into the next tree. They knew this would get the attention of the mother pig that would leave the brood and rush to the aid of her captured piglet.

At the same time, Rachel Lee would jump down and grab the runt of the litter. They all had decided that runts were supposed to be the smartest.

Henrietta had the job to jump down and hold open the cage they had fashioned for the runt. The two of them were to run as fast as they could down the hill toward the carriage road, leaving the boys to release the other captured piglet when the girls and their runt were out of earshot of the mother pig. The boys would then wait until the mother pig and her brood moved on.

The plan went like clockwork until Henry threw the piglet into the burlap blanket. The piglet got so scared it stopped squealing. Meanwhile, Rachel Lee reached for the runt and it started to squeal. The squeal got the attention of the mother pig which changed directions and began to run toward Rachel Lee.

Henry had to jump back to the ground and have the boys throw the piglet back to him. When the piglet hit Henry's arms it let out a squeal, jumped to the ground and ran toward his mother which had turned back toward Henry. She stopped to check her offspring giving Henry enough time to climb back up the tree.

Rachel Lee threw the runt into the cage and as each of the girls grabbed a handle they looked back to see Henry shimmy up the oak. On that cue the girls raced down the mountain with the squealing runt between them. Now that they knew he was safe, the vision of Henry scampering up the tree with the mother pig hot on his trail became hilarious. Peals of laughter mixed with the piglet squeals followed them as they ran down the mountain path.

The girls didn't dare stop until they reached the Reservation barn up the hill behind Bath House Row. That's where they were supposed to wait for the boys.

"Oh my side, it's killing me," Rachel Lee gasped as both girls dropped to the ground by the fence railing.

"Mine, too ... I can't breathe," Henrietta panted.

For a moment, the runt squealed in terror until it figured out it wouldn't be hurt. Then Rachel Lee and Henrietta's gasping and bouts of stifled giggles took command of the otherwise tranquil morning air.

After catching their breath and resting a bit they attempted to make the runt's acquaintance. But it would have nothing to do with them till they offered up a few kernels of corn.

"I think I need to go back up and see if they're okay," Rachel Lee said with a tone of concerned.

"I'll stay here," Henrietta declared. "I don't care to run into that mother pig again."

The girls heard the boys racing down the mountain before Rachel Lee took a step. She looked back at Henrietta and fell to the ground laughing. By the time the boys reached them both of the girls held their sides trying to breathe and laugh at the same time. Jake and Max joined in the fun and also fell to the ground. They didn't need to be told what was so funny.

Henry stood among them. "What's so funny?" he asked with clenched fists on his hips, knowing good and well what was so funny.

The others couldn't answer and Henry couldn't hold in any longer. He bellowed with laughter joining his companions on the ground his laughter expressed a mixture of joy and sheer relief to be out of danger.

After getting the merriment out of their system they turned to the business at hand.

"How long do you think it will take to train it?" Henrietta was the first to speak.

"Well, *it* is a *she*," Max, ever the farm boy, pointed out.

"Weeks, maybe months, I really don't know. What do you think Max?" Henry responded.

Everyone knew that Max was very knowledgeable about animals and even older people respected his opinion. His family ran a dairy farm on the edge of town and many of his father's customers lived in Hot Springs. Most Saturday mornings, before the sun arose he helped his father deliver milk. He often stayed with his friend, Jake, till his father headed home in the early afternoon.

"Since she is still young, I would say about six weeks to teach her the basics real good and get her to trust us. You know pigs are one of the smartest animals around," Max stated. Then he thought a minute and added, "But I don't know anything about truffles."

"That's going to be the easy part," Henry spoke with the confidence of someone who had known about truffles all his life, instead of someone who had recently become acquainted with the expensive culinary treasure. "It's going to be easy pickings."

In Rachel Lee's world, easy pickings didn't exist but Henry was good at figuring things out, and that was half the battle. His idea was that once a thing was figured out you could make a plan of action. Like a math equation, if you had all the parts to an equation, it could be figured out. What she admired about Henry is that he could always identify the parts to any equation.

"Albert, you know, one of the chefs at the Arlington," Henry continued, "said we could supply their kitchen and he would get me addresses of some hotels in St. Louis, Memphis and even Antoine's in New Orleans. So, all we have to do is come up with a good letter of introduction."

"We can get Miss Amber to type it up for us," Rachel Lee offered.

"Good thinking. Typing will make the letter look professional," Henry stated as he stood up resting one foot on the bottom rail, excited to lay out his plan.

"We're pretty sure we have a product, a way of harvesting the product, and a market for it."

Rachel Lee thought Henry sounded as though he were addressing a business association. As she thought about it that was exactly what he was doing. She and Henry were equal partners since it was their idea and their responsibility to get the operation going. Henrietta, Jake, and Max made up the third part of the partnership. It was their job to help out with tasks like catching the piglet.

"I've already made arrangements with Mr. Housley for shipping crates," Rachel Lee offered. "He's going to save all the smaller boxes."

"That's great," Henry commended. "Housley Brothers Mercantile is in the neighborhood, and they always have a lot of shipping crates."

"Papa said he would make sure our orders were put on the first train out," Henrietta announced.

"Now all we have to do is figure out how to get the truffles from your grandparents' property to the Cedar Glades post office," Henry pondered.

They had learned truffles lasted only a few days after finding them. Rachel Lee had agreed that for them to send fresh truffles directly to restaurants would be more profitable. And with trains running in and out of Hot Springs all the time their truffles would be in St. Louis, Memphis or New Orleans with time to spare.

"Well, kids," Jake spoke up adding his voice to the proceedings, "I think we need to give our piglet a name before we do anything."

"Anyone got any ideas?" Henry asked.

Names shot out right and left until everyone settled on Pinky.

"Pinky it is," Henry added his voice. "Well, I have to get down to the Arlington before the bathers come out. Although I don't think it's going to be worth the effort."

On Saturdays, Henry mainly sold newspapers to visitors, especially those going to their morning baths. But the smallpox scare kept most visitors away.

Having concluded the meeting everyone else stood up. Max and Jake took possession of Pinky. "We'll get her settled in," Jake assured his older brother.

"Grandmother said the churches are opening again tomorrow, so we probably won't be able to come by till after services," Rachel Lee stated.

It was the first time churches had held services since the epidemic started. The preacher probably would have a longer-than-usual sermon. But the Methodists always let out before the Catholics no matter what. Rachel Lee figured she and Henrietta could get home, eat dinner and have plenty of time before supper to go visit Pinky and the boys.

"See you tomorrow," Rachel Lee waived to Henry as he headed down the north path to the Arlington Hotel. She then turned to join Henrietta, the boys and Pinky. They had walked several feet in front of her, heading down the south trail that led to the Government Free Bath House and out to Central Avenue. But without Pinky to transport she covered the distance in no time and joined her companions.

Chapter 9

Cedar Glades Association

It was now late in May and school would let out for summer in another week. The family always spent summers and early fall time through the harvest season in the mountains near the village of Cedar Glades. It had cooler and fresher summer air than in Hot Springs. Whenever Rachel Lee thought of Cedar Glades she thought mainly of her grandparent's place, Journey's End Farm, and not the village itself. The family farm covered 160 acres called upland, because it sat high up toward the mountains and away from the Ouachita River. Her grandparents lived there when they first came to Arkansas from Virginia a few years after the War. It was about 2½ miles northeast of Cedar Glades village.

Usually, the girls and their grandmother headed to Journey's End Farm after the Fourth of July celebration, followed by their grandfather and Samuel in August. And they stayed through harvest time. The boarding house closed up except for Miss Amber. But as Rachel Lee had to keep reminding herself, nothing had been normal this year. Henry and Jake would make their first trip back to Cedar Glades this summer since their father died in a mining accident a year ago.

Mary would join them, also, along with Max and Pinky the truffle pig.

Pinky had begun truffle training. About two weeks ago, the Arlington Hotel received its first of the season summer truffles. After washing them off, Albert, the Arlington Hotel chef gave Henry a jar of the wash water. Henry used the truffle-scented water to soak his training cloth. After soaking five pieces of cotton cloth all night he balled them up and buried them about two to three inches deep around the oak trees in their back yard and left them there a couple of hours.

It was nothing for Pinky to pick up the truffle scent; the trick was going to be keeping her from eating the truffles. But Henry already figured out she liked corn better than truffle cloth.

At the moment, Rachel Lee and Henrietta sat quietly on the main stairway landing, right below the library. The quarterly meeting of the Cedar Glades Association had started. Mr. Stephens and Henry had been asked to join the meeting.

"I sure wish I could hear what they are saying," Rachel Lee whispered to her cousin.

"Me, too."

"And, I wonder why they asked Henry to come?" Rachel Lee continued.

Their friend had turned 13 recently, but he looked big for his age and that made him look a lot older. "Maybe they need his help with something. He could sure use the money."

"Yeah, he and Jake both ... with visitors staying away because of the smallpox, their paper business is down to nothing," Henrietta stated.

"For that matter, everyone's business is gone. That's why the association is meeting. I'm sure glad Mr. Worthington is now in the association," Rachel Lee said cheerfully. Rachel Lee's grandfather had talked highly of Lee Worthington. He was an investor looking for new mines. Dr. MacNeil made health visits among miners and had met Worthington through those experiences.

The girls talked softly. Their grandmother had cautioned them not to make too much noise during the meeting.

"If he's right about their being a lot of copper in the Cedar Glades area, it will mean more jobs." Rachel Lee added.

The original association members besides her grandfather were Thomas L. Martin, a merchant at Cedar Glades; Columbus Boone, the town's blacksmith; and Vander Housley who used to live in Cedar Glades but was now in the mercantile business in Hot Springs, right down the street on Ouachita Avenue. Uncle Samuel and Mr. Martin's son, John, a farmer in Cedar Glades, now had membership with Mr. Worthington and Mr. Kendall, a lumber man from Georgia.

She and Henrietta hadn't even been born when the association started in the mid-1880s during the mining boom. Back then, the association supplied lumber to the mining camps and to Hot Springs because construction also boomed during this period. Workmen built the Cedar Glades railroad line, too. Generally, it transported timber down from the mountains. Later, when the building and mining boom ended, the few miners left in the area became the main travelers on the association's line. They nicknamed it "The Cedar Glades Express," because the rails ran down from the mountains straight to the Ouachita River, running along its banks almost three miles and then turned back north, ending at the village of Cedar Glades. Rachel Lee remembered riding on the railroad handrail car once when she was little. She had never traveled so fast.

Henrietta, ever the impatient one, interrupted her cousin's thoughts. "I can hear grandmother and Mrs. Ellsworth fine. Sounds like they are close to the hallway, guess she is leaving. Let's scoot down and listen to what they're saying."

"You're right," Rachel Lee agreed, and started easing down the steps on her back side.

Usually it wasn't polite to listen in on someone else's conversation. Their grandmother had given them permission to wait on the steps for Henry. So they figured grandmother knew they were present.

The closer they got to the bottom step the clearer Mrs. Ellsworth's voice became. She had been visiting her brother, Mr. Van Patten. He lived down Prospect Avenue about three blocks away. Sometimes, after visiting her brother, Mrs. Ellsworth would stop by and visit with their grandmother.

"Sounds like she is having as much trouble with her garden as everyone else," Rachel Lee commented.

"I swear they keep coming by the millions," Mrs. Ellsworth angrily proclaimed. "The only way to kill those villainous worms is with a stick. I have planted twice this year already, and still all I have left is a suggestion of a garden to remind me of the labor I've expended. First the pigs, then the cutworms ... I don't know why I even bother, except I so wanted to have fresh vegetables when Frank comes home this summer."

Rachel Lee knew how dead serious Mrs. Ellsworth was, but she and Henrietta couldn't help but find humor in the way she put things. They almost giggled out loud when she said she had a "suggestion of a garden" left. And to picture stately Mrs. Ellsworth bent down attacking cut worms with a stick was really funny. But they didn't dare laugh out loud. Mrs. Ellsworth was a leading lady of the city. Their grandmother would become very upset if she heard them laugh out loud right now. It would be like laughing at Reverend Millford in the middle of his sermon.

They heard the Cedar Glades Association men moving around in the library. Henrietta tugged on her cousin's arm and indicated she wanted to go back up the stairs.

Since the voices in the parlor had moved to the hallway and trailed off toward the front door Rachel Lee didn't mind following her cousin upstairs.

The door to the library had opened and they could clearly hear Mr. Stephens speaking. "Henry and I will be happy to do all we can to assist you in the repairs. In fact, I'll enjoy working outside for a change," he said.

The girls saw Mr. Stephens talking to Mr. Housley and probably the other association members. "Pleased to have you on board," Mr. Housley shook his hand and took his leave along with the other members of the association. The men greeted the girls on their way down about the time their grandmother appeared from the hallway.

"Your grandfather wants you girls up in the library for a family meeting. I'll be up in a minute," their grandmother instructed before seeing the association men to the front door.

When the girls entered the library they saw their grandfather sitting at his desk and Uncle Samuel, Henry and Mr. Stephens gathered on either side of him. They were examining a map laid out on the desk top and looked as if they were in a deep discussion.

The girls quietly made themselves at home on the nearest chairs.

"All the tools are here at the rail barn," Dr. MacNeil stated, as he pointing to a place on the map. "You should be able to make it to the base camp in a day-and-a-half. From there it is only about a mile up to the rail barn."

At this point Dr. MacNeil and the others looked up and noticed the girls. "Come on over," their grandfather stated, "you need to know this too."

The girls squeezed in front of Samuel.

Rachel Lee had seen the map before, but now she looked at it with renewed interest since their grandfather wanted to show them something.

"Girls, you're going on a big adventure," their grandfather stated. As he spoke his finger tapped the map at the location of the rail barn. "The association has hired Mr. Stephens here to oversee repairs on the Cedar Glades line. With Mr. Worthington's mine operations expanding and Mr. Kendall starting up his lumber camp, the old Cedar Glades Express is going to need some shoring up. And, since the Craig brothers moved to Oklahoma last year the association has been without a clearing crew. Henry here is going to lend a hand. In fact, there will be work for you two and Jake and Max."

The opportunity to make money didn't come their way too often so they jumped at the chance.

"I guess with all the fires we've had the town is going to need a lot of lumber to rebuild," Rachel Lee offered her opinion.

"You're right, honey," Dr. MacNeil answered, patting his granddaughter's arm.

At this point Annie joined the others at the desk, facing her husband.

Dr. MacNeil gave his wife a smile and nodded then continued his announcement. "Miss Hurley has volunteered to go along and cook for the party, and to look after you girls and Jake and Max."

"We're all going?" Henrietta exclaimed in delight a split second before her cousin would have spoken.

"That's right," their grandmother interjected. "Miss Hurley has the next three weeks off since her new boss Mr. Leeman will be in New York on business. We thought this would be a good opportunity for all of you to leave town for a while and get away from the troubles. Mary and I, and, of course, Buttercup, will join you at the farm in a couple of weeks."

"And father and I will join the rest of you the first of July," Samuel added.

Rachel Lee couldn't help but notice that everyone sounded giddy, and she knew they wanted to escape as much as she did.

"We'll celebrate the 4th at the farm and get an early start on summer," Dr. MacNeil spoke gleefully.

"So everyone is going to stay the whole summer," Rachel Lee inquired.

"All of us," her grandfather smiled.

Her grandfather had not sounded this lighthearted in forever.

"Now," he continued, pointing once again at the map, "Let's get down to business."

Chapter 10

On The Road to Cedar Glades

Preparations for the big adventure went like clockwork. Everyone felt excited to leave town for a while. Rachel Lee loved Hot Springs, but winter blizzards, fires, the smallpox epidemic, and now the economic downturn that got worse became too much to bear.

Mr. Egner who owned the wagon yard down the street rented them a covered wagon and a team of horses. He offered a discount if they took Prince with them, as a summer outing away from the yard would do the old horse a world of good.

The old buckskin was past his working days, but Mr. Egner kept him around because he and everyone else in the neighborhood had grown attached to him.

Rachel Lee was beside herself. She thought of Prince as her very special friend. He had always been around, as long as she could remember.

Since the trip would take a day-and-a-half they decided to start their journey soon after the mid-day dinner meal. They could ford Glazypeau Creek by late afternoon and set up camp in the evening on the west bank of the Glazypeau.

The Cedar Glades party made their way through town, turned up Cedar Street from the Whittington and Central Avenue intersection, and then veered right, heading up Cedar Glades road in a northerly direction.

The wagon had the lead, with Henry driving, Rachel Lee next to him and Jake on her other side. Pinky rested in her cage on the floorboard beneath Jake's feet. Henrietta and Amber sat nestled inside the wagon and Max and Ethan followed in the rear—Ethan on Prince and Max perched on his mule, Jesse, in the middle of the pannier that carried the extra supplies.

The steady climb up Sugarloaf Mountain ended at the crest. "Whoa!" Henry said in a deep toned voice as he pulled back on the reins. This stopped the horses from going forward.

"Wow, I think I'm going to get off," Jake exclaimed. He scrambled down with Rachel Lee on his heels.

"Me, too!" Rachel Lee yelled.

The road leading down from Sugarloaf Mountain looked dangerously steep and made a decidedly sharp turn to the west. The last place Rachel Lee wanted to be was in a runaway wagon plunging headlong down a mountain.

"Steady there, good boy," Ethan had pulled up beside the wagon team to make sure they were calm and to assess the situation. "Henry, you take Prince. I'll drive."

By now, Amber and Henrietta were by the side of the road standing with Jake and Rachel Lee.

"I want to see," Max exclaimed as he jumped down from Jesse, handed Henrietta the reins and took his place at the crest of the mountain. "Oh man."

"Everyone get in the back. I'll see you at the bottom," Ethan ordered.

Rachel Lee thought he sounded a little unsteady but didn't say anything.

Max climbed back up on Jesse.

"Be careful," Amber implored.

"I'll follow and make sure he's alright," Henry offered and was galloping down the mountain before anyone could object. "They might need some help."

With that Jesse and his clumsy load plunged down the mountain after Prince, leaving Amber and the girls to walk the distance to the bottom.

"Well, thank goodness it sprinkled during the last two days," Amber said with a sigh of relief. Damp roads meant they wouldn't get choked with dust kicked up by Prince, Jesse and the wagon wheels.

The road continued at a steep incline for almost a mile before it leveled off any.

By the time they met up with the rest of the party the wagon and team had been thoroughly inspected. Everyone felt relieved that the trip down had not unsettled anything.

Amber and the girls climbed into the wagon and sprawled out to rest. Henry took up the wagon reins again. Jake, Ethan and Max returned to their places in the caravan.

After a short distance, the road again took a downward course before turning up and then down again. Another mile or so and they crossed Bull Bayou Creek. From there they traveled another three miles or so and reached Clear Creek. Here they passed the remnants of an old mining camp, refining plant and hotel. The buildings stood empty. Some had white curtains waving from hotel windows without any glass in them. They remained from the mining boom of the '80s.

Soon they turned north and reached the community of Hawes. The travelers stopped some distance from the Hawes store and sawmill to rest the team.

It had been decided ahead of time to keep to themselves, as the smallpox epidemic made everyone in the countryside nervous. Anyone coming from the direction of Hot Springs would not be welcomed.

What they found surprised them.

"I don't see anybody," Henrietta spoke first.

They all noticed the silent sawmill. The Hawes community had a general store with a lone horse in front of it. Otherwise the community had an eerie stillness about it.

After a few minutes, the whole traveling party agreed to move on.

For miles everyone chatted and sang; again enjoying the freedom of the open road. But now a pall came over the little group from the Market Street plaza neighborhood. Rachel Lee suddenly realized they had traveled a long way from the security of home and an equally long way from the safety of the farm.

In a shorter time than any of them wished, the sun had leaned far to the west. And they all knew Blakely Mountain to the west of Glazypeau Creek would claim it in another hour.

"I see the Glazypeau," Ethan shouted out in front of them and raced back to tell everyone the good news.

"Yahooo!" Jake yelled out in glee.

"We made it!" Rachel Lee exclaimed, a wave of relief sweeping over her and everyone else.

"It's not far at all. I'll go and scope out a campsite," Ethan announced.

As the wagon approached the campsite Rachel Lee saw that Prince lacked a saddle and now happily devoured lush clumps of grass while tied to a tree. She also noticed that Mr. Stephens had already re-arranged rocks where previous travelers had had a fire.

No one needed an invitation to set up camp.

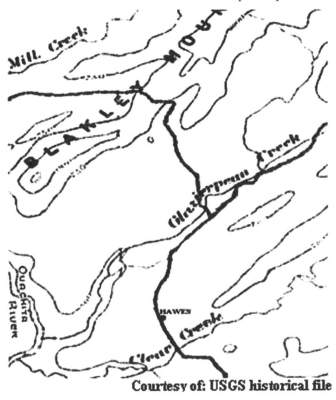

Courtesy of: USGS historical file

Henry and Ethan helped Max unburden Jesse and then they unhitched the team. Meanwhile Jake tended to Pinky, and by the time the animals were settled in, the girls and Amber had gathered wood and started a fire.

Everyone knew that dusk had set in and they moved quickly to set up the tents, one for the ladies and one for the gentlemen.

Half-way through setting up the tents an unexpected and eerie sound screeched through the air. "Eeeeee … eeeee!" Everyone jumped.

"What in the world …?" Ethan said as he dropped his tent line and jerked his head around to see what was making such a monstrous cry.

"Eeeeee ... eeeee!"

"There it is," Henry pointed upward toward a tall oak tree. "It's a great horned owl."

Henrietta and Rachel Lee instinctively moved closer to Miss Amber. Everyone else stayed silently glued in place, including the animals.

All eyes focused on the creature with the strange call.

"I'll bet he's at least two feet tall," Ethan responded.

Suddenly the bird leaped from his perch and soared across the camp. "Eeeeee ... eeeee!"

"Look at that wing-spread," Ethan spoke in awe. "It's got to be five feet long."

The strange call quickly faded through the trees. "Alright girls, we need to hurry and get this done and fix supper."

"Man, that was something," Max spoke in admiration for the large winged creature.

"I thought he had his eye on Pinky," Jake responded.

Max thought about that for a second. "I think Pinky needs to go back in her cage this evening."

Talk at dinner centered mainly on the great horned owl and what lay ahead of them the next day. The evening felt warm but their uneasiness caused everyone to sit a little closer to the fire.

"We best turn in early," Amber announced shortly after dinner.

There was no resistance to the idea as everyone had had a long day and knew another one lay in store for them tomorrow. Also, the idea of resting in a tent felt like a safer place.

The next morning when Rachel Lee awakened she thought her mind played tricks on her. She thought she smelled coffee and fish. The smell of coffee in the morning was usual, but not fish. Henrietta still slept but Miss Amber had awakened. She could hear Miss Amber and Mr. Stephens talking in hushed voices.

Her habit of stretching in the morning awakened her tent partner.

"Do I smell fish?" Henrietta asked, opening one eye and showing a puzzled look.

"You sure …" Rachel Lee started.

"Hey kids," a voice announced from just outside the tent. "Time to get up, breakfast is ready."

The voice outside was Jake's. He was the only person in the world who greeted everyone with *hey kids*—his brand of 'we are all in this together' greeting.

"We're up. Be there in a minute," Rachel Lee answered and scrambled to dress with Henrietta following suit.

The boys had begun eating by the time the girls joined the others around the campfire. Amber tended to the frying pan and Ethan wrote in his journal. The journal would help him with his report to the association at their next meeting.

"Good morning, grab a plate, these crappie are about done," Amber stated.

"Biscuits are over here," Henry offered.

"Crappie, that's my favorite, who caught them?" Rachel Lee asked

Ethan raised his hand and grinned, "I did. Didn't have any luck in the Glazypeau, but I found a pond just to the north of here."

After breakfast, the caravan broke camp and headed toward Blakely Mountain. They had a goal to reach the top by mid-morning.

The party spent the early part of the morning traveling with the wagon and horses to the base of Blakely Mountain. The caravan navigated a creek shoreline that led to a pass through the mountain. They followed the creek bed until it ran out and at that point everyone hiked up the mountain. The pine forest soon closed in on them. Rachel Lee started to notice that nothing stirred, not the trees nor any animals. The only sounds in the woods came from the lumbering wagon wheels with an occasional snap of a twig under foot.

The map Ethan carried indicated that the top of the mountain stood more than 1,000 feet high and they had started at around 500 feet. Where the mountain flattened at the top, the wagon stopped.

Ethan looked around from the wagon seat to see if everyone was accounted for. "I think that was the worst of it," he announced as everyone took up residence on the ground beside the road toward the back of the wagon.

The others moaned in agreement.

Ethan unplugged a barrel of water at its bottom and let it pour into a canvas water bag to quench the horses. Everyone else took turns with the dipper until they had their fill. After a few minutes of rest, the band of travelers gathered around Ethan to look at the map. All had great interest in knowing their location and how much farther they had to travel.

"We're going to go down here," Ethan pointed with his finger, "go around and follow along this ridge, then down to Mill Creek and then the river. Here is where the base camp will be; from there to the rail barn is maybe a mile."

"How long is that going to take?" Jake beat the others to the question.

"I don't know," Ethan pondered. "It's going to be slow going down the mountain. It'll take us maybe three hours to get to Mill Creek and a few minutes more to get to the river. We'll eat a bite, set up camp then catch our supper."

Everyone welcomed that bit of news. They all loved to fish.

"I hope I catch a catfish," Henry announced.

"Me, too ... a big one," Jake exclaimed.

"It shouldn't take us more than a half-hour to get to our base camp right here," Ethan tapped the map where the road, the Cedar Glades railroad line, and Blakely Creek intersected a few yards up from the Ouachita River. After a pause, he spoke again. "Alright, let's go."

Carefully, Ethan folded the map and the small gathering on top of Blakely Mountain prepared to make their departure for their final push toward the Ouachita River valley.

The ride down couldn't compare to the trip up the mountain. A mild wind from the river valley blew its way up to the tall pines.

Rachel Lee grew excited. When wind blew through the pine groves of the Ouachita Mountains it made a swishing sound like nothing else in the world. Not a whistling or a rustling, but a solid strong deep sound. She could feel its life, like God himself was speaking. That was her thought on wind blowing through Ouachita pine groves.

Unthinkingly, she sat up in the saddle and drew in a deep breath knowing that in the air there would be the distinctively faint scent of oranges given off by the pine needles. "You can smell it, too, can't you boy," Rachel Lee spoke and gently patted her friend, Prince, whose nostrils had flared in delight at the cool breeze.

Max still rode his Jesse, since only he could handle the animal. Ethan had decided to relieve Henry at the driver's seat while he took his turn to stretch out for a rest inside the wagon. Jake, Henrietta and Pinky kept Miss Amber and Ethan company up front in the driver's seat.

The journey down proved uneventful, to everyone's relief. In less time than Ethan had predicted, the pine forest fell behind them and now hickory and Blackjack Oaks began to spot the landscape. Rachel Lee thought Blackjack Oaks looked like the ugliest trees in the world. They always looked chewed on, their lower branches dead and void of leaves bending way down like they wanted to hide their trunk.

As they wound their way downward, other types of trees appeared, other varieties of oaks, and of course cedars in abundance along with dogwood, hackberry, walnut, maple, and mulberry. Rachel Lee loved the sweet taste of the purple-colored mulberries. They had a big one on the farm and it always had a lot of berries.

The closer they got to Mill Creek the thicker the vegetation appeared. They now saw untamed muscadine vines and wildflowers, huckleberry, blackberry, parsley hawthorn, and shrubs for which Rachel Lee didn't know the name. She couldn't name all the trees, either, but she had favorites that she recognized. She saw cherry, persimmon, redbud, sassafras, pawpaw, hackberry, plum, and the stately elms and lindens. Bees made the best honey from the linden blooms and her grandmother dried their blooms and used them as a medicinal herbal tea.

She knew that when they got to the low lying areas near the water she would see sycamores, ash, and willow in abundance. "They all have their place," Rachel Lee could hear her grandmother say. "If there were only one kind of tree in the woods there would be few animals, for each type of tree is both home and food to some type of animal."

The forest sounded alive again with chirping. The trees swayed and squirrels and chipmunks scampered at the rumbling of the wagon wheels.

"Look," Amber pointed down the road, "I can see an open field ahead."

The wagon lumbered into the open and rolled along Mill Creek for a minute or so and then stopped beside a patch of cane growing along the creek.

"We are going to need some poles," Ethan announced as he pulled to a stop. "Henry, hand me the hatchet. Everyone stay where you are. We don't want to stick around here long."

He didn't have to explain why. Bears liked to eat cane leaves.

Ethan cut enough cane for everyone to have a fishing pole and a few extra in case one broke or found itself in the river. After tossing them to Henry along with the hatchet they started back down the road and soon arrived at the site of their base camp.

ON ROAD TO CEDAR GLADES
Courtesy of Garland Co. Historical Society

Chapter 11

First Night in Camp

The river appeared as wide as Market Street plaza and in some places dark blue where the water was deep, and lighter blue in the shallow places like between the sand bar in the center and the sandy bank on the other side.

"Henry, would you bring the cooling chest out as you come?" Amber requested. "I think the ice is almost gone and we need to finish off the rest of the milk and what is left of the cheese and ham."

"I'll help," Jake offered his brother a hand.

The cooling chest was a metal lined, thick white oak wooden box, made to set flush with the front part of the wagon frame just inside, behind the seat. The good location made it handy to grab when climbing in and out of the front of the wagon.

The base camp, as Ethan called it, sat right where the rail line turned north for a mile, toward the mining camps. In the other direction the line headed west for about three miles then turned north to Cedar Glades for half a mile.

As Rachel Lee understood Ethan's job, he had to assess the winter damage and clear the gravel ballast road bed and side ditches of undergrowth and debris. The side ditches measured 20 feet in width on each side of the road bed. The Craig brothers had taken care of the line for years so it wasn't overgrown. But the line looked shaggy. The crew would have lots of chopping of vines and trimming of trees—a job that needed the work of everyone in the party. And, as it also would mean a lot of bonfires along the railway, she knew they would have some fun times, too.

Ethan also had to check the cross ties, wooden rails and iron straps on top of the rails for damage, then map out a work sheet for the association's repair crew. The Cedar Glades Express ran on top of iron straps that had been attached to wooden rails. The rails had been laid about five feet apart and on top of cross ties that were 10 feet long and spaced a few inches apart. Each rail had been built two-and-a-half inches wide, seven inches deep and 12 feet long and placed in notches in the cross tie. The cross ties rested a few inches apart from each other.

The Cedar Glades Line differed from the ones back east and in Canada, due to the type of wood used—all cedar for the ties and rails. Everyone said it would last a lifetime. The straps made of iron fit over the top of the rails. Each strap stayed in place with nails that had to be countersunk to keep the surface smooth.

The Cedar Glades clearing crew ate a small meal then set up their tents. They also raised a tarp on poles so its edge stood just outside the campfire. The tarp would provide shelter for cooking in case of rain.

After finishing the last of his mid-day dinner, Ethan pulled the pot of boiling water from the cooking grill and poured the hot water into the milking pail, swirled it around and threw it out. "I think before we do anything else I need to go across and get some milk," he announced with his newly cleaned pail in hand.

They all heard the lead milk cow in the distance across the river. She wore a five-inch-long, four-by-three-inch rectangular copper bell on a leather strap collar around her neck. Any farm knew the rhythmic clang-clang like routine background music. This particular Jersey belonged to one of the farmers that Dr. MacNeil contacted about getting milk.

Everyone wanted to help get the milk, not so much for the milk, but so they could ride the raft across the river.

"Go ahead," Amber spoke lightheartedly, "I'll hold down the fort. Go ... go," She mockingly shooed everyone toward the river. "I'll string the poles, but you're going to have to get your own worms when you get back."

Everyone scrambled toward the raft. Large ropes had been threaded through metal rings along the rail on each side of the raft and looped through pulleys anchored on both sides of the river. A pull on either rope freed the raft to cross the river to the other side.

Ethan handed Rachel Lee the pail. "It's stuck in the mud; we need everyone's weight on this end," Ethan stated. Everyone moved to the far end of the raft away from the bank. Ethan and Henry pulled on the ropes and they lunged forward, forcing the river's current beneath the raft and rushing out the other side. "Hold tight to the railing," Ethan commanded.

The further out the raft got the swifter the current. On shore it hadn't looked fast at all, but Rachel Lee and the others realized the river was moving very rapidly.

"I see fish," Jake pointed downward.

"They're schooling … right size for bait," Max offered.

"I'll take your word for it," Henrietta squealed, hanging on for dear life and regretting her impulse for adventure.

Ethan and Henry were too intent on getting them to the other side. But Rachel Lee could see the shiners. "Hey, there's a big one, looks like a black bass," she called out.

They had passed the mid-point of the river and the current slowed down, making it easier to see into the water.

"Wow," Rachel Lee exclaimed while looking at several large catfish deep in the clear calm water, "this is where we need to fish."

The boys agreed. Henrietta still occupied herself with her own survival as Henry and Ethan made their final tugs on the rope.

Suddenly the raft thumped against the far bank. "Everyone to the other end," Ethan commanded his crew, then stretched out his arms, grabbed both ropes, and pulled hard, landing his end of the raft onto the sandy beach.

The cows gave a passing glance at the action on the river and then returned to grazing. The cows were used to humans which was why they took little note of Henry and Ethan's approach.

Rachel Lee and the others stayed with the raft. Max and Jake had already waded into the water. Henrietta removed her shoes and sat on the side to place her feet in the water. Rachel Lee kept an eye on the boys and another on Henry and Ethan.

She could see through the trees at the edge of the field that Ethan had already started milking. Henry held the cow's collar making sure she didn't move. It also positioned him to stand guard in case a bull decided to view them as encroaching on his field.

In no time he had filled the pail, but their walk back took a long time because Ethan tried to avoid spilling any milk. Their backs were to the cows so they didn't see the bull charging across the open field toward them.

Rachel screamed as she jumped from the raft. "Behind you, a bull …. a bull …. run!" Frantically, she waived her hands. The others joined her at the fence line screaming and waving their arms.

Ethan not daring to look back dashed awkwardly toward the screaming banshees with his pail of milk. Henry suddenly changed course and ran to his left then stopped and turned, waving his arms and yelling at the bull. This maneuver stopped the bull in his tracks just long enough for Ethan to reach the fence hand the milk pail to Rachel Lee and crawl through the fence.

Rachel Lee stood paralyzed with fear for her friend. This was no pig; it was a full grown ornery bull.

The hefty creature now chased Henry who moved in a zig-zag pattern toward the tree line. This slowed the bull down as Henry could turn quicker than the bull. Everyone held their breath knowing they couldn't do anything with the bull this close. In a flash, Henry reached the tree line, jumped up, and grabbed a low lying limb, allowing his forward motion to swing his legs forward; the momentum propelling his legs upward into the tree. The bull screeched to a halt, snorted while rolling its head in anger, its horns coming dangerously close to the limb that supported Henry.

Possessed with relief, Rachel Lee and the others fell to the ground with peals of laughter at the absurd drama that had unfolded before them.

The bull soon wandered back to his cows and Henry joined them in their merriment. "And I thought the mother pig looked mean," he said as he crawled through the fence.

After catching their breath they made their way back across the river where Amber anxiously waited on the bank.

"Good heavens," she exclaimed, relieving Rachel Lee of the milk pail and addressing Ethan and Henry,

"I heard all the yelling and saw that bull charging you and I'm here to tell you it aged me 10 years."

It was a toss-up as to whose version of the story Amber heard since everyone talked at once.

Even after they had all caught their share of fish and finished supper, talk around the campfire continued to center on the bull charging Ethan and Henry.

Before they knew it, dusk settled in and a chill crept into the camp. Ethan made a move to add more wood to the fire. For a moment the campers were transfixed by the leaping flames.

Henry broke the silence. He addressed Ethan, "Say, how about telling everyone the story you told the association. You know, the story your grandfather told you about the railroad at Harper's Ferry and the Great Train Raid of 1861."

Rachel Lee could tell he didn't need any coaxing. She thought it must be one of his favorite stories.

"Quickly, gather around," Ethan motioned. "I need to draw this out before it gets dark so you'll have a picture of where the railroad was."

As everyone crouched closer Ethan took a stick and drew some lines in the dirt, made some Xs, and scrawled out some letters next to them. "You see right here?" He pointed with the stick as he spoke, like a professor lecturing on the War Between the States.

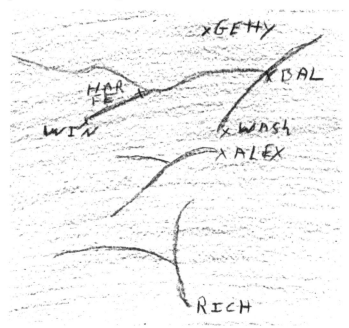

"It started back in the early 1830s when the Baltimore and Ohio railroad line was created by some northern businessmen. They decided to build a railroad right across the northern end of the rich farming region of the Shenandoah Valley so that they could ship all the products from this area to the northern ports."

"Where is the Shenandoah Valley?" Max and Jake asked at the same time.

"In Virginia, mostly, and a little in West Virginia," Amber volunteered.

This satisfied the boys so Ethan continued.

"The Virginia General Assembly didn't waste any time chartering the Winchester and Potomac railroad. It connected with the B&O railroad at Harper's Ferry and ran south, right into the Shenandoah Valley for 32 miles to Winchester. But the railroad wasn't authorized to connect to any railroads further south because these northern businessmen didn't want all the products from this area transported and shipped out through the southern ports."

"Because it would take business away from them," Henry observed.

"That's right. The northern and southern ports were in competition with one another. And I guess the businessmen in Pennsylvania, Maryland and Ohio had more political pull than the guys in Virginia.

"What do these letters stand for?" Henrietta asked.

"Well, up here to the north is Gettysburg. Down here to the right is Baltimore and across to the left is Harper's Ferry and Winchester to the south. Washington, D. C., is to the south and east. Across the Potomac River is Alexander and due south is Richmond."

Ethan paused a moment to let everyone familiarize themselves with the geography of the area where his story took place.

The last ray of light evaporated into darkness and everyone gathered back around the fire to hear Ethan's story.

"Twenty-five years later, in 1859, old John Brown and his band made a raid on the federal arsenal at Harper's Ferry, Virginia … now in West Virginia. You remember, he was an abolitionist and thought he would go south and stir things up."

Rachel Lee had looked up the word abolitionist in the dictionary once even though she knew what it meant and how to spell it. But she wasn't sure how many syllables it had. According to the dictionary it had five syllables, but the way some people she knew pronounced it she thought it might have had more.

"Well, Brown and his raiders ended up trapped in the engine room of the arsenal, with hostages. Colonel Robert E. Lee, who was in charge of the Marines that guarded the federal arsenal, was ordered to arrest John Brown and his men. You know, General Lee was an officer in the United States Army before the war."

Everyone nodded their heads that they knew.

"Colonel Lee and his men charged right in there and arrested the whole bunch of them. But rumors started flying from the south that the Winchester and Potomac railroad was going to be used to rescue Brown and his men from the gallows and up north they were all worried the W&P was going to be used to invade the north. So the Governor of Virginia took military control of the line."

By now, a roaring and crackling fire illuminated the camp. Croaking tree frogs and insects of the night gave a blended backdrop of sounds as Ethan's voice continued the talk.

"When war broke out in '61, there was even greater concern on the Union side that the W&P railroad would be used to send troops up north, since it connected to the Baltimore and Ohio line. But what the southern boys had in mind to begin with was to use the W&P to start moving machinery from the Harper's Ferry arsenal down to Winchester, and then transport it further south by wagon into the Confederacy.

"The man who had been the Chief Engineer for the W&P railroad, Thomas R. Sharp, was a friend of my grandfather. Captain Sharp served in the Confederate States Army under General Stonewall Jackson in what they called the Railroad Corps.

"Soon after the start of the war, General Jackson and his men rode up north on the W&P and raided the B&O. You see, the South didn't have many factories so they ended up having to borrow a few things from the north."

Ethan grinned at his last remark and stirred the fire with his stick before resuming his story.

"First, Jackson and his men burned several locomotives and over 300 railway cars belonging to the B&O line. They were under Union control and he didn't want them used against the south. Then he took control of a section of the B&O and several more of their locomotives and at least 80 railroad cars.

"But now came the ingenious part. Jackson had his men take apart four small locomotives, the kind used on the strap-rail lines like the Winchester and Potomac railroad; mounted them on special dollies and wagons. It took 40-horse teams to pull them down south."

"Forty!" Rachel Lee, Max, Jake, and Henrietta all said at once, like a chorus.

"Yeah, 40," he said. "Then he had them reassembled and placed on tracks at Strasburg. That line connected with the Virginia Central and the whole Confederate railroad system.

"Once they knew it could be done they continued to help themselves to other engines, cars, rails, ties, and machinery of all kinds," Ethan stated.

"Man I would have loved being in the Railroad Corp," Jake announced, his eyes wide open eager to hear more. "What happened then?"

"Well," Ethan continued, "the Union boys took over the W&P in the spring of '62. But by then, most of the confiscated goods had already been sent south to the Confederate railroads. So our boys didn't have any need for the Winchester line. However, when the north decided they wanted to build a railroad making a circle from Washington, D.C., to Shenandoah Valley, Jackson had his men burn the main W&P's bridges and tore up the entire track. After Jackson and his men left, the Union Army repaired the track. Then the southern boys thought it might be a good idea to go back and take up the new track, but they didn't have enough wagons so General Lee had them destroy it again."

"That must have been the most laid-down and torn-up track in the country," Henry remarked.

"And that wasn't the end of it," Ethan continued. "In the first part of 1863, there was another battle for control of the northern Shenandoah Valley. It was called the Second Battle of Winchester. The Southern army once again took all the rolling stock they could get their hands on as well as tools and machinery."

"What's rolling stock?" Jake inquired a second before Rachel Lee.

"It's locomotives and cars mostly," he answered and continued on with his story. "Here's the kicker, sometime during all this tearing up and rebuilding of the W&P the Union forces decided to remove the strap rail and replace it with T Rails, like most railroads today. The iron strap rails were placed in storage at Alexandria, Virginia, and eventually sold at auction. Now here we are 30 years after the war and the owners of the Winchester and Potomac railroad still have a case before the federal court against the U. S. Government, demanding to be paid for the loss of their strap rail. Can you believe that? The federal government has been fighting that railroad claim for 30 years."

Everyone agreed that was remarkable indeed.

"But it still doesn't beat the government's court battle to claim our thermal springs. I think that holds the record. Let's see, the federal government set the Hot Springs area aside in 1832. But people had been living around the springs for years and many of them claimed they owned some of the property the government now claimed. They went to court and fought over the springs and surrounding area till 1876 when the Supreme Court had their say. That would be 44 years," Ethan concluded, standing up and holding back a yawn.

For a minute or so everyone stared in the fire thinking of railroads and raids.

Rachel Lee suddenly realized how tired she was and figured it was bedtime. "I'm going to bed," she stated simply and stood up to leave, then turned to Ethan. "That sure was a good story."

"Well, thank you," Ethan replied.

The others agreed and everyone else stood up having decided to turn in for the night as well.

"I'll bank the fire," Henry offered.

"Everyone needs to get a good night's rest. We start work tomorrow," Ethan stated.

Ethan's parting words didn't have any effect on Rachel Lee. After the long trip and everything that happened today she knew she would sleep well.

Chapter 12

Clearing the Tracks

As planned, they broke camp the next morning and headed up to the rail barn.

"It looks pretty deserted," Amber said as they reached the clearing at the end of the line.

"We'll start clearing away from the barn before we tackle the tracks," Ethan stated as he and Henry pulled open the doors.

Rachel Lee noticed that the barn doors had notches at the bottom to fit close to the railings. Inside, the main track ended in an arrow shape with connecting track to the left and right. The rolling stock sat there. All of the cars used hand or horse-power. The barn had two horse-drawn gravel cars the miners used for their ore, three horse-drawn flat cars for the lumber men, a hand repair car and another hand-car used for inspection. They planned to use the hand-car. Wooden animal stalls stood on either side of the barn. At the back running the length of the barn was a room for tools and extra supplies to repair the tracks.

Ethan turned to Amber and spoke, "From the looks of things, I think we will be camping here tonight. But no matter how far we get down the track today I think it's best to re-locate back to the base camp tomorrow.

We'll have the hand-car then and we can leave you, and the girls and the animals in camp."

The wind blew from the south so everyone decided it was best to build their brush fire toward the back of the barn and set up camp on the south side close to the opening.

All hands pitched in to clear away the brush from around the barn and then started cleanup on the track. They stacked another brush pile further down the track to burn later. No one cared to have smoke in their face all night.

By late afternoon everyone had tired from their first day of chopping, cutting and stacking.

"Did anyone else hear that cat last night?" Max asked the next morning.

"We both heard it," Jake added.

"Yes, I heard it," Ethan answered. "I thought you two were asleep.

"We were afraid to move," Jake confessed.

No one else had heard it.

"Was it what I think it was?" Max asked.

"Yes," Ethan responded, "it was a panther."

"A panther!" Amber exclaimed, horrified at the thought.

"Now don't worry, they don't want to run into us any more than we want to run into them."

Ethan spoke with such confidence that he relieved everyone of their fears.

After breakfast, they loaded the tools they would need onto the hand-car and headed back to their base camp. Henry and Rachel Lee provided the manpower for the car. Ethan and Amber rode in the wagon. Prince and Jesse had halters on ends of ropes that tied to the back of the wagon.

"You're going to have to go slow, we don't want a loose strap to flip up and hit any of you," Ethan cautioned as they headed out.

The trip back to camp was great fun even though they wished they could have gone faster. The next day was a day of rest as it was Sunday, and outside of fishing and exploring along the banks their time was spent blissfully whiling away the day.

The next day, the boys and Ethan worked on the line north of the camp and the girls and Amber did what they could to clear away the smaller brush and debris from the roadbed close to camp. Ethan had already started his repair report for the association, too.

By their fourth day out from home the Cedar Glades Express, workers had established a routine. Ethan and the boys headed out on the hand-car every morning chopping underbrush and trimming tree limbs all day along the right-of-way and returned in the late afternoon. Every other day, the girls and Pinky would ride with them, getting off first to clear small vegetation along the rails. Usually it didn't take but half a day to reach the choppers. Some days though, the choppers made better headway when there wasn't as much underbrush which meant the girls had more ground to cover.

After their mid-day meal, Henry and Ethan went back to work while the others explored the countryside. Occasionally, the others had to check the brush fire and stoke it. The time spent in the countryside proved to be ideal for looking for truffles.

A crude map was soon drawn to mark the truffle areas in case they found any, so they would be able to find them again when their job for the Cedar Glades Association was finished. It wouldn't be too hard to find the marks on the map because fields and orchards lay beyond the tree line and those made good landmarks.

Amber took care of the camp, did the cooking and spent part of her days reading the novel she had brought along. For several days she had kept her eye on a bramble clump and one afternoon she surprised the others with a blackberry cobbler for desert.

"Maybe tomorrow I can take Prince and check the road for more berries," Rachel Lee offered. Rachel Lee knew Henrietta would not want to pick blackberries, as she had never mastered the technique of picking berries without getting scratched by their prickly stems and leaves.

Amber gave her approval. By mid-morning the following day Rachel Lee and Prince sauntered happily along the road westward toward Cedar Glades in search of blackberries. The open space near the rail line gave way to woods, but soon opened up again. The berries grew in abundance in several fence lines along the way, but she and Prince were enjoying their outing too much to stop. There were many fields of crops and three different orchards along the fence-line to their left. She knew the Ouachita River lay beyond the fields, but trees and underbrush blocked it. All the corn crops had grown about a foot or two in height and the hay fields looked ready for a first cutting in a week or so. To their right the Blakely Creek ran parallel with the road for almost a mile and then it turned north. At this point she entered a wooded area on both sides and decided to turn back after going a short way.

"Guess we should pick some berries before it gets any later," she spoke softly to Prince.

They stopped at a couple of places she had mentally marked along the way, and could have filled her bucket at any of the stops, but she had fun picking the biggest ones and moving on. There was one more place she wanted to stop before heading back to camp. It was a few yards from the first woods she had entered, and she knew it had really big berries along this section of fence. At this point, the road closely followed Blakely Creek and became steep. Rachel Lee tied Prince to a bush that grew close to a strip of red clover on the creek side of the road. She walked over to the other side and climbed up the embankment to find the berries.

She hadn't picked five berries before she heard the fearsome spine tingling cry of the panther. The sound came from a rise ahead of her down the road in the woods.

Prince made a pitiful whinny sound, yanked his tether rope loose, taking part of the bush with him and ran head long into the creek, leaped to the other side and disappeared in the brush.

Rachel Lee knew she stood alone with the panther. She froze and didn't move a muscle. The only sounds came from water gurgling in the creek and her heart pounding in her ears. The panther let out another cry. It had come closer. At this Rachel Lee acted on pure instinct. She threw down her berry bucket and dashed across the road, jumped into the creek and made a bee line for the place she had last seen Prince. Another cry followed her across the creek, but she didn't dare look back. Suddenly, she heard an awful high pitched whinny and the crashing of horse's hoofs. She dropped to the ground in sheer terror and turned to watch as Prince reared up at the edge of the creek and let out a savage scream that caught the panther off guard and stopped him in his track. Again, Prince pawed the air and the large light-tan cat turned and ran away.

"Oh, Prince, you came back!" Rachel Lee cried out, tears streaming down her face. It was unclear as to which one of them was shaking more. Gently she stroked his neck and talked softly taking comfort in his massive frame. "You're the best Prince; you're the best horse in the whole world." And then she started sobbing and buried her face in his neck.

Understanding his young friend's relief and gratitude he let out a soft whinny and bobbed his head in response.

"Come on, let's get those old berries and get back to camp," she said wiping her face. "I don't think the panther wants to tangle with us again, but I'm not going to test him out."

Chapter 13

Home to the Farm

After the panther incident everybody stayed close to camp or the work area along the rail line. By Tuesday of the following week, they had reached that section where the rail line turned north.

A gate separated the last half-mile section from the rest of the line. It could be easily opened, but remained closed to keep in the cattle on the other side. This section of the line was kept up by the local farmers whose property bordered either side.

Late Wednesday morning, the road crew packed up their base camp and after the mid-day meal, headed north to Journey's End Farm. Rachel Lee rode Prince with Henrietta as their passenger. When the young riders eyed the pasture leading up to their grandparent's homestead they could hardly contain their excitement.

"Hang on!" Rachel Lee yelled for Henrietta to hear. Rachel Lee persuaded Prince to spring past the wagon and galloped down the lane toward the house.

Their grandmother and Mary tended to a late planting in the vegetable garden. Hearing the sound of a galloping horse they both moved to the edge of the garden and peered down the road. Buttercup had already started at a dead run toward the caravan, barking with delight.

"It's the girls!" Annie exclaimed.

Both the women crossed to the front porch to greet the riders.

"I see the wagon, too," Mary added.

Buttercup reached the girls and greeted them with hearty yelps.

"Buttercup!" They squealed in delight.

"Hey, boy," Rachel Lee greeted their four-legged friend.

"Good Buttercup. We sure have missed you," Henrietta announced to the smallest member of the family.

Prince slowed to a fast walk and then stopped before the welcoming committee.

"Grandmother! … Aunt Mary!" the girls exclaimed as they slid down from the saddle, embracing first one then the other.

"Have we got some stories to tell!" Rachel Lee started as she bent down to hug Buttercup.

"You won't believe what all has happened," Henrietta continued.

Before they could launch into a story the wagon came to a halt and hugs and greetings continued.

Buttercup got a whiff of Pinky and moved toward the wagon to investigate.

"Did you bring the boxes from Mr. Housley?" Henry asked his aunt.

"Of course we did," Mary responded.

"Come and have a seat on the porch," Annie offered. Annie put her arm around Amber. "I know you're glad to be off that wagon."

"You can say that again. I think it bounced around everything I own," she said holding her stomach.

"Anyone for sweet cider?" Mary asked.

Everyone responded with a resounding "yes!"

"The children are dying to tell me everything that's happened," Annie addressed Ethan and Amber.

"That might take a while. Think I will tend to Pinky and the wagon and horses," Ethan offered good-naturedly.

Henry automatically started to go with him.

"No, Henry," Ethan motioned, "you need to stay here and defend yourself."

"Thanks," Henry responded with a grin.

Everyone gathered on the front porch and when Mary had returned with the sweet apple cider it was decided they would all take turns, and that Miss Amber could start the tale of their adventure with their troubles getting down Sugarloaf Mountain on the first day out.

Ethan returned a few minutes later and offered his account of their journey to the river.

Some of the stories got funnier with the telling. When Rachel Lee told of the panther incident, it got more frightening on review. But she and everyone else understood the art of storytelling. Making the panther sound bigger and Prince more ferocious made for a far more colorful and entertaining story.

"Pinky located a couple of truffle sights already," Henry pronounced proudly.

"So, now, you think the wee little Pinky might soon be earning her keep," Mary teased.

"We'll find out soon that's for sure," Henry promised.

The Truffle Association had put high hopes on Pinky. They had all agreed that most of the money they had made working for the Cedar Glades Association would be used for start-up cost in their truffle business—mainly postage. It had also been agreed upon that after expenses, half of the profits from the sale of the truffles would go to help out each family, and the rest divided between the partners. This made everyone feel grown up to think they could help their families out financially. Especially since they knew that with the winter blizzards, the fires and now the smallpox epidemic, everyone in Hot Springs was financially strapped.

As there was no shortage of stories, the Cedar Glades crew entertained Annie and Mary until late in the day.

Rachel Lee knew as she sat there on the front porch of her much loved Journey's End Farm that she would remember for all her life the adventures of the Cedar Glades clearing crew. The cheery voices of her best friends and closest family mixed sweetly with the song of the distant whippoorwill, heralding the end of day.

She felt good to have done her part to help get the Cedar Glades Express up and running.

"And after a good night's sleep," she thought to herself, "Henry and our truffle association will embark on our first truffle harvest tomorrow."

Glossary of Terms

Abolitionist — Someone who campaigned against slavery in the 1700s and 1800s.

Alley Taw — Marble used as a shooter.

Ballast — Gravel or stones used as a foundation for railroad track.

Banshees — In Irish and Scottish folklore a spirit of a woman who wails to signal that somebody in the household is going to die.

Epidemic — Outbreak of a disease.

Euchre — Card game.

Escargot — Pronounced ĕs'-car-gō'. An edible snail.

Feral — Wild animal.

Great Horned Owl — A large North American Owl with large ear tufts.

Inoculation — To introduce a weakened form of a disease into the body in order to create an immunity to the disease.

Jersey — Light brown dairy cow that produces good cream.

Morris Chair — Armchair that reclines at different angles.

Mycology — Branch of botany that studies fungi.

P's and Q's — Old expression that means, "be on your best behavior."

Pannier — Either one of a pair of baskets hung across the back of a mule, horse, etc. Sometimes made of wicker.

Panther — Large light tan cat found in mountainous areas of the western hemisphere.

Piglet — Young pig.

Quarantine — To isolate in order to avoid the spread of disease.

Roquefort	—	Pronounced rōk'-fert. Sharp-flavored cheese with bluish mold, made from sheep or goats milk. Originally made in the French town of Roquefort-sur-Soulzon.
Shenandoah Valley	—	Valley between Blue Ridge and the Allegheny Mountains, in western Virginia and eastern West Virginia.
Shiners	—	Small silvery freshwater fish.
Strap Rail	—	Wooden railroad lines of the 1700s and 1800s topped with a strip of iron.
Transom	—	Small rectangular window over a door.
Truffles	—	Pronounced trŭf'-el. An edible, potato-shaped fungi that grows underground. Located with help of either pigs or dogs.
Vaccination	—	Inoculation with a vaccine to create an immunity.

National Historic People and Places

Antoine's Restaurant-
New Orleans restaurant established in 1840 by Antoine Alciatore. Originally Antoine Alciatore along with his wife, Sophie Freyss Alciatore, established a boarding house and restaurant. The name Antoine's Restaurant was adopted in the late 1860s. It continued as a boarding house for several years after the Civil War.

John Brown-
1800-1859, American abolitionist who led raid on the federal arsenal at Harper's Ferry (1859). Hanged for treason.

Martin Eisele-
1853-1944, Hot Springs, Ark., pharmacist, superintendent of Hot Springs Reservation (what became Hot Springs National Park), 1900-1908.

Brigadier General Robert E. Lee-
1807-1870, Commander of the Army of Northern Virginia. Feb. 6, 1864, appointed General-in-chief of Confederate forces.

William J. Little-
Hot Springs, Ark., businessman and superintendent of Hot Springs Reservation (Hot Springs National Park), 1893-1900.

Winchester and Potomac Rail Road-
Shut down on authority of Virginia governor in connection with Brown's raid in 1859. Confederacy used W&PRR to ship machinery from Harper's Ferry arsenal to Winchester, Va., 1861 to January 1862. Used by Confederacy during the "Great Train Raid of 1861," and then seized by Union forces in 1862. Iron strap rails removed, stored in Alexandria, Va., and later sold. Rail replaced by T rails.

U.S. Supreme Court

United States v. Winchester & Potomac R. Co., 163 U.S. 244 (1896)

United States v. Winchester and Potomac Railroad Company, No. 195

Argued March 31-April 1, 1896

Decided May 18, 1896

163 U.S. 244

Syllabus

The Court of Claims had no jurisdiction over this case, as the claim of the defendant in error is a "War Claim," growing out of the appropriation of property by the army while engaged in the suppression of the rebellion.

This appeal brings up for review a judgment in favor of the Winchester & Potomac Railroad Company, for the sum of $30,340, the value of certain iron rails removed in 1862 from the track of that railroad by the military authorities of the United States.

In 1896, the United States Supreme Court ruled in a lawsuit that overturned a previous judgment in favor of W&P Railroad Company for $30,340 for the value of the iron rails that were removed in 1862 during the American Civil War. The W&P Railroad Company claimed that its stockowners were loyal citizens during the war, and that the United States had taken possession and control of the valley up to Winchester, and then had removed its strap and T rails over to the Manassas Gap Railroad for service and storage in Alexandria, Va., and they were never returned. Furthermore, W&P Railroad had paid Manassas Gap Railroad $25,000 in 1874 for rails that had been put on to the W&P Railroad.

City Business Directory

Selected Businesses from 1892 and 1897 Hot Springs, Arkansas

—**Arlington Drug Store**, 184 Central Ave.

—**Barry, Dr. Wm.** Health officer, 516 ½ Central Ave.

—**Barry Hospital**, 4 Water St.

—**Eisele & Hogaboom, Martin A. Eisele, Ed Hogaboom, Logan J. Hunt, drug store**, 184 Central Ave.

—**Ellsworth, Prosper H.,** physicians, 234 ½ Central Ave.

—**Fitzsimmons, Mrs. M., proprietress, Alhambra Hotel**, 117 Ouachita Ave.

—**Gray & Housley (Fred Gray and John W. Housley),** dry goods, 664 Central Ave.

—**Harrell, Martin L., physicians**, 745 Central Ave.

—**Housley & Lakenan (Evander T. Housley and William A. Lakenan),** general store, 112 Ouachita Ave.

—**Ledgerwood Bros (John J. and James E.),** bakers, 222 Ouachita Ave.

—**Little, Wm. J. Mercantile Co. (William. J. Little, president; George P. Kennan secretary,** general store,
    605 Central Ave.

—**Post Office Drug Store**, 802 Central Ave.

—**Rockafellow, Charles N.,** bath house, 12 Park Ave.

—**St. Joseph Infirmary,** 1 Cedar Terrace.

—**Van Patten, S. P.,** architect, Gaines block.

Hot Springs, AR., City Directory Advertisements, 1892 and 1897

The Alhambra Hotel.

RATES, $7 to $15 PER WEEK.

Commercial Travelers' Headquarter

GOOD SAMPLE ROOMS.

MRS. M. FITZSIMMONS, Proprietor.

117 Ouachita Avenue,
Opp. the Famous Alhambra Bath House.   HOT SPRINGS, AR

1892 Hot Springs City Business Directory
Courtesy of: Garland Co. Historical Society

TURF EXCHANGE | TRACK ODDS on RACING EVENTS
Telegraph Connections With All Tracks

1897 Hot Springs city Business Directory
Courtesy of: UALR Archives

Hot Springs, AR. *The Visitor*, Feb. 23, 1895

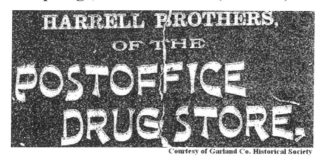

HARRELL BROTHERS,
OF THE
POSTOFFICE DRUG STORE.

Courtesy of Garland Co. Historical Society

METEOROLOGICAL REGISTER.

Station Army & Navy Gen'l Hospital, Hot Springs, Ark, Month February, 1895

DAY OF MONTH	TEMPERATURE			PRECIPITATION				GENERAL DIRECTION OF THE WIND
	MAXIMUM	MINIMUM	RANGE	TIME OF BEGINNING	TIME OF ENDING	TOTAL PRECIPITATION	DEPTH OF SNOWFALL	
1	42	x 14	28	11 a.m.	4 p.m.	.1	Snow 1 inch	N.E.
2	40	x 10	30					N.E.
3	44	x 16	28					N.E.
4	54	x 18	36					S.
5	48	x 16	32					E.
6	40	x 20	20					N.
7	46	-11	57					N.
8	36	x 14	22					N.W.
9	Observations mislaid							
10	39	17	22	1 a.m.	12:30 p.m.	.6	Snow 6 inch	S.
11	42	22	20					N.W.
12	46	17	29	Light snow during night				N.
13	35	12	23					N.
14	33	20	13					N.
15	43	23	20					N.E.
16	47	23	24					N.
17	48	23	25					E.E.
18	60	27	33					E.E.
19	58	35	23					N.
20	58	23	35					S.N.
21	67	38	29					N.N.
22	63	38	25					S.E.
23	60	35	.25					S.E.
24	67	31	36					S.N.
25	71	52	19					S.N.
26	71	47	24	PRECIPITATION VALUES				S.N.
27	76	46	30	Comp. by M. L. Garrant				S.E.
28	70	48	22	Date 2-18-42				S.E.
29								
30								
31	"a"							
TOTAL	1404					.70	7.0	
MEAN	52.6	temp't used						

x mean p't't used

Remarks: The minimum thermometer was out of order and cannot be depended upon for these dates, the lowest was probably from -3 to -6.
No loss of life or property by lightning known

Surgeon U. S. Army

Hot Springs City Council Meeting Minutes, March 22, 1895

The following bills - approved by the Board of Public Affairs.

C. E. Harrell & Co. Vac. Points R		$35.47
Dr P. L. Barry, Services		100.—
Dr J. C. Minor, "		100.
Dr E. M. Remmington, "		50.
Dr T. M. Band, "		100.
T. W. Mitchell, "		14.
And the accounts of		
Joe O'Bright Services		13.
Pay Roll - Special Police		134.38

Were on motion of Ald Babcock Allowed and ordered paid.

The Salt Lake Herald, "Experiments Now Being Made With a Serum," 11 February 1895

ANTI-SMALLPOX.

Experiments Now Being Made With a Serum.

St. Louis, Mo., Feb. 10.—Since the appearance of smallpox two weeks ago, experiments have been made secretly at quarantine to manufacture an effective smallpox serum that will obtain the same results in its branch that anti-toxine has for diphtheria. The experiments are under the direction of Health Commissioner Homan, and Dr. A. N. Ravall, of the Washington University. These two men have materially been aided in their work by a series of tests made last December at the quarantine station at New York by Dr. Elliott. On the basis of these experiments, Dr. Ravoll at once set to work two weeks ago and vaccinated a strong, healthy heifer with baccilla, taken from a smallpox patient. After the animal had sufficiently recovered, he took some of its blood and extracted from it the serum. The first actual tests were made only three or four days ago, so that the results, whether favorable or otherwise, cannot yet be learned.

Three Strangers Come To Call — 2008

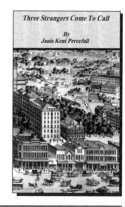

1895 was a time when people throughout the United States traveled to Hot Springs to bathe in the thermal springs as part of what was known as the water-cure. Eleven year old cousins, Rachel Lee and Henrietta encounter three strangers intent on meeting their grandfather, Dr. Robert MacNeil, a local physician and Civil War veteran. Each stranger presents their grandfather with a gift: one shocking, one a pleasant surprise, and another not wanted at all.

"...brings 1895 Hot Springs to vivid life"
— Liz Robbins, Director - Garland Co. Historical Society

$16.00 - 131 p. - Historical Fiction - Juvenile
Showcased at the 2010 Arkansas Literacy Festival

Ouachita Springs Region: A Curiosity of Nature — 2006

A false impression was gained in some way that this hospital was erected for the indigent sick of the country, with the result that our city was infested with paupers from every state in the Union, hoping to gain admittance to the "government hospitals". We wish no such impression to get out regarding the City Dispensary.

The Hot Springs Medical Journal - February 1895

"a most honest and, therefore, refreshing account of how Hot Springs became the Nation's health resort...a powerful book because it challenges a myth...more than a commentary on the healthcare of a century ago...lessons to be learned in our present generation's attempt to grapple with the issue of federally sponsored health care for all Americans". - Ouachita Life Magazine

$19.00 - ISBN: 9780615137384 - 198 p. - w/Index

---

18 x 24 Full Color Map depicting the Villages of Buckville and Cedar Glades in the Ouachita River Valley during the 1890s

$10.00 plus $5.00 S&H

Books & Maps may be purchased at: OSRHRC - P.O. Box 3032, Hot Springs, AR 71914
Please add $2.00 per Book and $5.00 per Map for Shipping & Handling